GOLDEN ROD

Bram Riddlebarger

CABAL BOOKS
ST PAUL, MN

GOLDEN ROD

Cover design by Matthew Revert
Typeset by Michael Kazepis

Cabal Books
DBA Thicke & Vaney Books
P. O. Box 16305
St. Paul, MN 55116

For Pretty Girl

Up in Blood, where the tipples and the smoke and the heaps of slag stink and seethe, where tongues run slick and filmy from coalgas, the dead hand of man sits gray and hideous, and the frail planet is splintered.

DON ROBERTSON, *Paradise Falls*

PROLOGUE: MERLE HAGGARD

Merle Haggard's early recordings play throughout this narrative. They are the soundtrack of *Golden Rod*.

THE FORD'S DEMISE

Jack unsealed the gas canister and stepped up to the truck. The ghost of Sid hovered thirty yards away, beneath the branch of a fallen apple tree. The gasoline emptied from the rusted red metal like the Platonic Ideal of a golden arch.

Jack flicked a match, tossed it, and ran like hell.

The Ford exploded.

That was fast, Jack thought, as a shockwave of energy pancaked him to the earth. A rain of herbal tea ashes floated on the breeze. Plastic milk jugs scattered across the meadow like the bloated Civil War dead in a Mathew Brady photograph. Broken, Smurf-blue truck parts embedded themselves at unnatural angles in the earth. Fire spewed forth. The sound of a Hammond B-3 organ pulsed through the ghost of Sid's canine ears, and he remembered the lupine life, and then he quickly forgot it again, because it was almost time for supper.

As the oil fumes and the paint polluted the air and the burned-out hull of the truck smoldered down into art, Jack and the ghost of Sid embarked on their new life as wild, free-ranging locavores.

For Jack, it was a reaffirmation of his Yellow life.

For the ghost of Sid, well, he would soon meet himself.

THE YELLOW

The cool autumn weather increased the amount of herbal tea that Jack drank, but not by much. Jack already drank a lot of tea. The only time that Jack wasn't drinking tea was when he slept. Even then, a cup of tea cooled beside him on the floor by his sleeping bag.

The Yellow, as Jack referred to it, had begun to show up the week before. At first, there was only a strange glow, like a bruise, but then there was the Yellow.

Jack stopped by the Walls of Knowledge Library after his dishwashing job to search for answers.

He checked the usual things that there were to check in a causal relationship that ended in a yellow-hued penis. STDs. Jaundice. Infection. Cruel, though often funny, sophomoric pranks with dye. His diet.

Back home, hot water spilled from Jack's rust-red teakettle. The water was like a gray rainbow that led to a terrible pot of gold. Rose hips paired with spearmint didn't matter. If vanilla and chamomile embraced, only Yellow remained.

"Peter Piper pondered a yellow pecker," said Jack, five times fast. "Peter Piper pondered . . . shit."

Sid looked at Jack from beside one of the cold brown heaters that didn't work in the dining room of Jack's rented, run-down shack.

Jack opened his wallet. A receipt for dog food and a one-dollar bill lay in the fold.

Jack stewed in his tiny kitchen. Diatribes and vilification flew about like birds of frustration and hate. As any good bird-dog would do, Sid watched them and pointed when necessary.

Jack asked his friend, Tommy, about his condition.

"Hey, Tommy," said Jack. "You ever hear of a guy's dick turning yellow?"

Jack and Tommy both washed dishes at the Sandstone Hills restaurant.

"Yellow?" said Tommy.

They had finished their shifts and were hanging out at Tommy's place. They were watching the Travel Channel, seeing places that they would never go.

Jack drank from his designated teacup, while Tommy put away a six-pack of High Power in less than half an hour.

"Never mind," said Jack, "I gotta take a leak."

Jack hovered over the child-sized urinal that was attached to the wall in Tommy's bathroom, next to the toilet.

Tommy's wife believed in a world where gender equality constituted no piss splash on the walls of her ever-clean bathroom tile.

Tommy installed the child-sized urinal because he believed that men did not sit down to pee, and because a regular-sized urinal was just too big to fit.

It was a hard compromise.

Jack washed his hands.

He had permanently borrowed *The Outsiders* when he left the library, but Jack had no intention of staying gold.

"See you, Tommy," said Jack.

"Leaving?"

Back home, Jack brewed his tea and thought long thoughts.

"This goddamn Yellow," said Jack.

Sid looked at Jack from beside the worthless heater.

Jack stared back at Sid.

"Shit," said Jack.

He drank his tea.

And then he drank more.

THE HERBAL TEA BANDIT

Jack sat behind the wheel of his Ford Ranger. The truck was parked in a small clearing on Wang National Forest land, just off an old access road: garish blue against a backdrop of green and brown and yellows and red.

Thought had not been easy for the last month of Jack's Yellow life. Like pregnancy, his body had switched on autopilot and now attempted to betray him at every turn.

Sid pressed his nose against the passenger-side window of the truck. In his dog brain, Sid pondered the Platonic Ideal of opaqueness inside the cold, Smurf-blue of the truck cave. And then he thought of food, because there wasn't any around.

Jack stared through the windshield. His minimum-wage dishwashing job, Tommy, and all thoughts of medical assistance had succumbed to the Yellow.

Jack now lived on herbal tea alone.

His house with no heat had become a truck with four tires and a black aluminum cap.

Home sweet truck.

Since the forfeiture of his lease on the rental, Jack's best idea had been the creation of a wooden bed. The bed expanded his Ford bachelordom like a bleak horizon. Jack built the bed out of 2x4's and a sheet of 3/4" plywood that he stole from the landlord's shed behind the no-heat shack.

"Jesus, Sid," said Jack, as he made off with the lumber. He danced a land mine dance of dog shit across the yard.

Placed in the bed of his truck, the pilfered sheet of plywood created a two-storied living space. The top half became Jack's bedroom. He stored his meager possessions on the ridged metal below. When Jack slept, he often felt like he was living in a movie about space travel, where humans had to live well beyond their years in a small compartment in order to arrive at some troublesome destination.

For Jack, that destination had come.

The cab of the Ford served as Jack's pantry and dining room. He kept his boxes of herbal tea on the front passenger-side floorboards of the cab, wrapped in plastic grocery bags. Jack collected the bags from the sides of the roads in the county, where they blew like money from an armored car.

Jack drummed his fingers through the film of dust on the dashboard. He sipped his tea. On the hood of the truck, plastic milk jugs with tea bags crammed down their mouths warmed in the yellow sun. Toxins leached out of the jugs into the tepid water and then into Jack once he drank the tea.

"I need to boil some water," said Jack, extracting a nail from the board of his mind.

Jack got out of the truck.

"C'mon, boy."

Sid followed Jack to a small pond that was close to the clearing where Jack had more or less permanently parked the truck. Jack dipped a milk jug into the pond and filtered it through an old t-shirt into another jug. Back at the truck, Jack fashioned a dog harness out of some old socks and a piece of rope. Sid could haul two, gallon-sized milk jugs of pond water strapped to the harness. Jack carried four jugs. Six milk jugs of water equaled close to five gallons of tea.

"I think I might be able to carry six tomorrow," said Jack, after the angels took their share.

Jack had spent his last paycheck from the dishwashing job on a large cache of Wild Berry Zinger herbal tea. The Zinger had been on sale that day at the local supermarket:

**BUY ONE
GET ONE
FREE**

"Man, Sid, this Wild Berry Zinger kicks ass."

Sid didn't care.

Sid pressed his nose against the window of the truck, leaving another wet dog-nose print to dry onto the stratified layers of past dog-nose prints. Jack set his empty travel mug in the Ford's cup holder and stepped outside to pee.

The hills of Wang National rolled like leaf money.

Jack grabbed a full-gallon of brewed Zinger from beneath the Ford and climbed back into the driver's seat. Two empty milk jugs sat between Sid and Jack. Jack picked up his travel mug, poured it full, and capped the gallon.

"Make sure I put those empties out after I finish this jug, okay, Sid?"

Sid pretended not to hear him. Through the dog-snot window, Sid pointed at a dog-snot bird.

Jack stepped back out of the cab. He poured another half-gallon of pond water into a carbon-coated metal camp pot and placed it over the fire. To support his herbal tea lifestyle, Jack had been burning timber at a rate akin to the production of pig iron. He kept three soot-covered metal camp pots simmering over the fire, like charcoal, throughout the daylight hours.

Inside the cab, Jack drank his tea.

Whatever lay ahead of Jack in life was almost gone, unless it was bad.

The days rolled by.

The Ford didn't move.

Soon, Jack's ample supply of firewood became another problem. In addition to no visibility through the dog-snot window, the passenger-side door of the Ford could no longer be opened. Like a landlord for college students or low-income families, Jack was not practicing fire safety. He did not have an escape plan or a fire alarm attached to the aluminum ceiling of his bedroom. He had also built his fire pit too close to the truck, which was now encircled by wood. Between bouts of herbal tea euphoria and trips to the pond, Jack and Sid would roam the hillsides of the county and drag any deadfall they found back to the truck. Blackberry vine-like tangles of wild branches lay stacked like elbows around the Ford, as if Jack were attempting to build an ill-advised wigwam with no regard for how close his fire pit burned to a large pile of combustible wood and gasoline.

Jack placed a handful of Zinger teabags into a boiling pot of water, took it off the fire, and watched the colors seep out.

"*The stee-ping!*" sang Jack, falsetto, like a hair metal rocker in 1987.

Jack had had no viable nutritional sustenance for weeks.

His daily consumption of herbal tea had reached a new high.

The information on the boxes of tea clearly explained that additional food was required for survival.

Jack climbed back into the Ford's cab with his tea and immediately pissed himself.

"Goddamn," said Jack.

Sid sniffed and looked out the window.

"Stand proud, you people of wet days! The righteous will prevail!" Jack shouted, as his jeans became heavy.

He sipped his tea and tried to clear his mind.

Midas' reign, he thought, *rather than coming to a conclusively solid ending, has devolved into inglorious liquidity.*

Leaving a trail of piss drops dribbling behind him,

Jack slogged his Zinger-saturated jeans to the Walls of Knowledge Library. The time had come for further research. He stopped near the front steps of the library and read the inscription carved in concrete relief above the archway of the library's grand wooden double doors:

THE GATES OF KNOWLEDGE SHALL BE OPENED UNTO YE

"Sid. Wait."

Like a false prophet, Jack pulled open a brass-handled door and walked in. His shoes squeaked on the marble floor, as if it had rained that day. Every patron in the library began reading a pamphlet on the primordial animal instinct of Fight-or-Flight. An off-duty Lawman with military training had read this pamphlet many times before. The Lawman broke from a nearby magazine rack, tumbled three times across the hard marble and a thin carpet, and tossed Jack back out the double doors in one beautiful, continual motion. The front walk of the library transformed from rough-swirled concrete into a large, open latrine into which unwanted book browsers and homeless, piss-stink patrons were systematically and judiciously thrown.

Jack stood up, dazed but unsurprised, and began to limp back to the Ford.

He needed tea.

The hallowed realm of the bibliophile poured over with that favorite of leisurely ablutions, he thought, as he stepped from the concrete latrine.

Then he noticed the pack of wild dogs.

Jack ran, but it was no use. His last thought before the pack reached him was: *it's time to change my pants.*

Then the dogs set in.

Sid sat on the library lawn, waiting. As the dog pack affixed themselves to his master's lower extremities and Jack screamed, Sid watched with keen, yet traitorously detached emotion. Sid was every writer and philosopher in the world. Sid was Thomas Hobbes, Friedrich Nietzsche, and a wolf without a pack.

A three-year-old boy returning a *Curious George* book joined the screaming from the front steps of the library.

The off-duty Lawman heard the commotion. He ran to meet the danger.

"Dirty dogs!" the Lawman yelled, as he gunned down the pack without warning.

A student volunteer at the library called 911.

After the ambulance arrived to carry Jack off to the hospital, a squirrel crossed over the street on a power line. The squirrel and the power line were like an electric ballet. The squirrel hopped over to Sid.

"What happened here? I heard there was a fight."

"Yeah, they just carted Jack off."

"Jack-off? That the guy that lost?"

"Yeah," said Sid.

"Damn, I wish I'd been here to see it, but I was too busy

with my nuts."

Sid trudged back to the Ford, as the wild pack of dogs began to rot under the bright, yellow sun.

A MONOCHROMATIC KALEIDOSCOPE IN THE HANDS OF A FOOL

Two orderlies wheeled Jack's punctured body into the emergency room. They had Jack strapped down on a foul-smelling gurney. The grody gurney bumped across the metal threshold of the Only Hospital Around.

Maybe I won't have to pay, Jack thought.

The doctor saw the Yellow peeking out of the shreds of Jack's jeans.

"Huh," said the doctor.

The RN trainees from the local technical college raised their eyebrows, but the professional staff didn't blink.

A little yellow, a little trauma, pain, shock, delirium—these things come to pass.

"Sedate him," said the doctor.

"Does he have a highlighter pen in his pocket?"

As the clockwork of the sedative closed around him, Jack focused on tea.

The Promised Land, he thought.

The clockwork of the sedative struck twelve.

The drugs melted away.

"Uhhh," said Jack.

The room was white.

"I need some tea!"

The words echoed and bounced against the white hospital room and the cheap curtains and the stainless steel bed rails, and off the flashing, muted television set.

Jack's teaoholic hands trembled like the earth.

Zinger, thought Jack.

He surveyed the canine damage.

The Yellow was still there, intact.

A nurse with golden hair knocked once and opened the door.

"Hospital beds, you are prisons without bars," sang Jack, baritone.

The room spun like a monochromatic kaleidoscope.

Merle Haggard, who was singing a chorus, stopped.

"Quit interrupting me," said Merle. "But that's pretty good."

"Fine," said Jack.

The golden-haired nurse was unfazed.

"I could use some tea," said Jack. "And a bathroom."

"There's a urine bottle on the side of your bed there. Hanging on the rail. I've just got to check your papers. You should be okay to leave soon," said the nurse, like a breathtaking sunrise.

Jack could hear the Zinger calling from the floorboards of the Ford.

"We don't seem to have an address for you, Mr. —?"

"Yeah," said Jack. "Zinger. Chamomile. Ginseng—whatever you have."

"What?"

A yellow bloom spread across the white skin of the sheet. The urine bottle hung on the bed frame like an appendix.

At least I have health care, the nurse thought.

She grabbed clean sheets and a new gown from a cart in the hallway and headed back to Room 116, but Jack had left the building.

"You can only wring so much piss from so many pants," sighed the nurse.

She had dreamed of being a ballerina as a child, but now she had two kids at home.

Jack limped back to the wilderness of the Ford shrouded in the discolored sheet from Bed 116B. He had tossed his gown. Visions of hot herbal tea filled his head. Bittersweet phantom-aromas wafted on the winds ahead of him, beckoning him home to tea, Sid, and the Ford.

It was a long, cold walk back to the truck. The fall leaves had fallen.

Sid smelled him coming, upwind.

The golden boy.

Sub-master Jack.

Well, I hope he likes those smells, thought Sid.

After the library debacle, Sid had meandered back home to the Ford. Once there, he climbed the woodpile, crossed the hood, and jumped through the open driver's side window. He curled up in a ball on the passenger seat and sank into dog depression. His inherent loyalty to the alpha pack leader waned. He laconically pulled fleas, ticks, and burrs from his coat, and then he peed on the seats. He only left the truck once to lap cold Zinger from an abandoned metal camp pot beside the fire pit.

A day is forever without the pack.

During the lonesome hours, Sid pondered life. His prime years of rover hey rover come on over had passed him by, and his offspring were not many. He was hungry.

His job was not done.

Depression sat on his canine shoulders like the lost chance for an afternoon walk amplified by eternity. In a final act of canine rebellion, Sid pooped where he slept.

Then he smelled him.

Jack.

Happiness mixed with guilt like a one-night stand, and Sid's tail began to wag. He couldn't help it.

Hello, fecal Ford. Welcome to Lake Ranger. The seats are a little wet today, buddy, but the fishing is great.

Jack climbed in.

"Jesus, Sid. We're gonna have to burn this fucker."

Jack climbed out. Sid followed. They both let loose— Jack and Sid's Micturating Melody in P#.

It was teatime.

THE RANGERS-IN-DANGERS

As the stitches from the dog attack festered and discharged a familiar yellow shade of trouble, Jack lay on his plywood bed in the Ford thinking final thoughts. He had sealed up the cab and moved his remaining possessions to the bed of the truck.

"This is it, buddy," he told Sid.

Before the end, Jack brewed one hundred and seventy gallons of Zinger in a monumental last-ditch effort to go out with the tea.

"It's a little watery," said Jack, "but it'll do."

He stored the brew in four, fifty-gallon neon-blue plastic trash barrels that he stole from the Hollow Oak Cemetery.

These barrels will blend right in with the truck, thought Jack.

Before Jack and Sid liberated them, the barrels averaged eighty-one complaints a day from the quick and the dead.

"I sure don't miss those neon-blue trash barrels," said a man, walking beside his sister in the cemetery.

The siblings were there to visit the graves of their ancestors. The man carried a plastic flower that would last for several years, and the woman carried grief.

"Is that a ghost?" said the woman.

Jack and Sid were dragging the barrels into the woods. Jack had fastened two of the barrels to Sid's dog harness. Jack still wore the bed sheet from the Only Hospital Around, like a poncho, and his skeletal frame was ghostly.

"I could use a beer," said the woman, to her brother.

"We better get some High Power."

After the siblings rambling police report, paranormal investigators descended on the cemetery like Mothman swooping from the trees in 1966, but no conclusive paranormal evidence was ever found.

"Yep, everyone here is dead," said the Final Investigator.

The Lawman accompanying the investigation radioed in to dispatch.

"Yeah, we're about done here. Hey, you know of any meetings I missed? No? Okay. Yeah, I'll ask him."

The Lawman turned to the Final Investigator.

"Hey, you ever play the game Risk?"

Jack stationed the four barrels just below the rear back window of the Ford's cap on the driver's side. He had burned through most of his firewood brewing the tea. His escape plan was clear. From inside the bedroom compartment in the back of the truck, Jack could lower his travel mug through the mesh screen of the window via a t-shirt pulley into the waiting barrels. After picking out the organic debris that settled at various stratified layers throughout the tea like a righteous James Hutton, Jack drank. Two and a half barrels of tea remained. The odor of piss filled the air. The native wildlife signed away the rights to Wang National for fifty yards in all directions of the Ford epicenter, mineral rights included. The agreement gave Jack inalienable, inexorable, and absolutely incontrollable rights to that land until the grasses withered and the mountains fell down, which, being Appalachia, they mostly already had.

The United States government balked on the deal. Ten U.S. Forest Service Rangers in the latest biohazard and chemical cleanup suits purchased with post-9/11 Homeland Security funds appeared at Jack's rear window several days after the breakdown in negotiations.

"What's up, bud? What's going on here?" said Ranger One, as he tapped on the cap's back glass window with his Full Size Maglite.

Inside the Ford, Jack sipped his tea and stared at his aluminum ceiling.

"Grab the dog," said Ranger Two.

Sid looked at Jack, then at the Ranger's outstretched, nitrile gloves.

"Here, pooch," said Ranger Four. "Come, boy."

Feral instinct took over. Sid growled and lunged. After significant biting, scratching, and tearing at the federal taxpayers' expense, Sid took to the hills.

THE WILT CHAMBERLAIN PRIZE

Sid ran until he could no longer hear the sirens.

Then, he ran more.

The medevac buzzed overhead.

Sid began to look for food.

After chasing a few deer, Sid caught the scent of a pack of coyotes and ran farther still. He crossed a state route and bypassed a house with barking dogs. He slept in the woods. When he couldn't find anything to eat, he pulled grass stems with his front teeth and then puked them back up several hours later in a puddle of bile. Sid didn't smell it at first, but after a week of this new life, there was a new scent in the air.

Like many travelers, Sid had taken to searching the roadsides for food. He had found a few fast food morsels among the plastic bags that week, and also a very rotten deer carcass, but that was it. Then he smelled it. Chicken.

Sid followed the scent. In the pasture of a chicken farm, thirty or more chickens pecked around inside an electric fence. Several hens had escaped. Sid caught one by its tail and carried it into the woods. After that first taste of Golden Comet, Sid began feeding on chickens from the local farming community with wild abandon. He lurked in the woods and grew stronger. He earned the name "Sid the Proud" from his stray and chained-up peers alike. It wasn't long before the collective-anarchist group:

a mutt-like group of free-thinking and free-loving canine-radicals determined to gain control of the international food supply, awarded Sid the honorable Wilt Chamberlain Prize.

Sid roamed the woods.

He ate chickens, and they tasted like freedom.

Then Sid met the Revolutionary.

The Revolutionary had come to sit in on a DogsUnite! meeting and lend his moral support for all things revolutionary. He left with a new pet: Sid. Together, Sid and the Revolutionary raided the local chicken coops and slept in the woods. Together, they were free.

"Canines, comrades, whatever," said the Revolutionary.

Sid gave his best impression of a wolf and howled.

The Revolutionary, of course, yelled, "Canines of the world, unite!"

They really liked each other—the Revolutionary and Sid.

"Too bad my name isn't Nancy," said the Revolutionary.

THE GHOST OF SID

Jack stepped out of the psychiatric ward a year and a half after his arrest. He carried two possessions, one of which was an opaque plastic milk jug that he had used like a long-haul trucker throughout his incarceration. The milk jug dangled from his synapse-deadened fingers and smelled bad. Jack had named the jug during his time in the ward. He had drawn two eyes and a puckered mouth on one of its sides with a black permanent marker.

was scrawled above the two eyes, as if each letter of the word were another mangled bang in a bad haircut. Upon his discharge, a nurse handed Lemon, wrapped in a plastic hazardous waste bag, to Jack with a mixture of sorrow and disgust and unfettered, chortling glee.

"Here's your trophy, big boy," she said, exactly.

"Here's your marker back," said Jack. He pulled the black marker from the butt crack of his donated pants and handed it to the nurse.

The nurse dry-heaved and placed the marker into another plastic hazardous waste bag. She handed the bag with the marker back to Jack and threw away her disposable gloves. She squirted a blob of hand sanitizer into her hands from the bottle on the counter between them.

"Just call him 'Sharpie,'" said the nurse, who perhaps should have been in charge of the entire ward.

Jack slid the marker into the pocket of his pants and left the building.

Outside, the sun was shining and it was a new day. The sky was blue. The clouds were loony bin white. The close-cropped grass was a vision of chemical green.

"C'mere, boy," said Jack, to the ghost of Sid.

The ghost of Sid sat near the entrance to the building. A large puddle of ghost drool had formed on the sidewalk in front of him. While the real-life Sid roamed the woods, proliferated, and ate chickens, the ghost of Sid panted away in front of the psychiatric ward for one and a half long ghost years, patiently waiting for Jack like a ripening trust fund.

The ghost of Sid floated after Jack.

Jack and the ghost of Sid walked toward the far end of town. During Jack's incarceration, new big-box stores had risen up out of the ground like gob piles in the hills of consumption. Jack had not had a drink of tea in all this time.

But the Yellow remained.

"Maybe the Ford's still there," said Jack.

The ghost of Sid wagged his tail, but the air didn't move.

"I could use a cup of tea," said Jack.

Merle Haggard was singing.

RISK

Once or twice a month, the Rangers and an assorted group of lawmen, bankers, and freewheeling drifters would come together to play the board game Risk. These Thursday night games had a spaghetti-western quality to them, specifically of scenes set on a dusty Main Street, or in a chandelier-heavy saloon with a dry piano and plenty of whiskey. There was a rogue quality to the group that went unspoken, and the Rangers were invariably responsible for digging a hole in the county hinterlands on Wednesday night near an old, decrepit fire tower or some other lonely bastion of neglect.

"Do it, do it, do it," chanted the Saber Rattler, for the thousandth time.

"Let's make a treaty," said a freewheeling drifter, to Ranger Two.

Ranger Two had just taken over Asia.

The freewheeling drifter, like every freewheeling drifter, had just blown into town. No one knew where these freewheeling drifters came from. They rolled across the landscape like dice across a game board.

This particular freewheeling drifter held a strong block of the three countries just across the land bridge into North America. It would take some rolls of the dice, but the freewheeling drifter was as doomed as the giant sloth. His only hope was to skirt the rules and propose a verbal treaty somewhat outside the specified rules of the game, but within a gentleman's agreement of sport. Ranger Two had plenty on his plate. Asia held power, but there were enemies at every gate. He had no time to piddle away his bonus armies on the freewheeling drifter's large army while sacrificing his numerous fronts with Australia, Europe, and Africa. North America could wait.

"Okay," said Ranger Two. He moved a portion of his troops off the North American front to shore up the rising threat from Australia.

"If you can't be smarter, just be more subversive," said the Saber Rattler.

Grumbling and heavy drinking commenced around the table.

Dice rolled. Bitching and moaning ensued. Little plastic men moved around.

"Hey, remember that time you blew away all those dogs at the library?"

"Ho, ho, yeah."

"Yer turn, buddy."

"Pack of fucking wild dogs," said the Sheriff. "At the

library. Jesus."

Everyone at the table laughed and a few clapped the back of the still-off-duty Lawman, who was basking in the glory of the number of rounds that he had been able to fire.

"Mr. Library."

More laughing.

"'Dirty dogs!' I screamed."

"Lot of paperwork though."

"Yeah, lot of paperwork. But damn!"

The freewheeling drifter took a beating in Alberta. He took a beating in the Northwest Territory. His little plastic cannons were lost. His not-very-stable plastic cavalry pieces galloped off the playing board all too soon. O, fortune. The trio of attacking die was handed to the freewheeling drifter.

"Yer turn, bud," said a Lawman.

The freewheeling drifter held few cards. In Risk, a player must take over a minimum of one country per turn in order to receive a playing card that will eventually reward the player with numerous bonus armies. After his losses in Alberta and in the Northwest Territory, the drifter's options were limited for initiating offensive maneuvers. The other players had wisely buffered their defenses. Verbal treaties did not always sit well on Thursday nights in America. Only the weakened Asian province of Kamchatka held promise. The freewheeling drifter placed his few plastic infantrymen in Alaska, readying himself for his strike across the Bering Strait and thereby voiding his verbal oath to Ranger Two on the very first go-round.

"Kamchatka," said the freewheeling drifter, sealing his

fate.

Ranger Two bludgeoned the freewheeling drifter with his Full Size Maglite until the drifter's brains were on the floor. The freewheeling drifter would never reach Kamchatka, or any other town again. Despite the melee, only three wobbly plastic cavalry horses fell over on the table, but the game was over. Alaska held the plastic yellow infantrymen of a dead man.

"You dig that hole?" asked the Sheriff, once the drifter had stopped twitching.

"Yeah," said Ranger Two.

"Well, put him in it," said the Sheriff.

"Goddamn treaties," said a Lawman.

"It's a well-named game," said the Saber Rattler, for the thousandth time.

"Wild goddamn dogs. Jesus," said the Sheriff.

MELONS

Mental awareness returned as Jack walked away from the smoldering remains of the Ford and into the woods. He carried what few possessions he had salvaged from the truck in his hospital bed sheet. He threw Lemon away and picked up a much cleaner empty milk jug from the clearing. The world had gone wrong, but it was now made clear.

O, the colors so pure.

After a year and a half in the psychiatric ward, Jack decamped to the mid-summer countryside. He would live off the land. He would become a locavore. He thought that he could grow melons, and maybe corn, too.

I'll kill a deer with a knife, thought Jack. *I'll jump down from a tree limb and feast.*

Far down in the earth, something rumbled, but Jack didn't hear it.

"Sid. Here, boy!" yelled Jack.

The ghost of Sid had vanished.

Melons, thought Jack. *Sweet, round melons.*

The ghost of Sid reappeared and bounded happily along in the clean, Ford-less air.

Maybe melon tea, thought Jack.

Jack and the ghost of Sid began to search for food.

HIGH POWER

"Let's get some Brush Lite," said a local.
   "Yeah, that sounds good."
   "Nah, let's get High Power."
   "Yeah, that sounds even better."
   The locals went to buy some beer.

UNCLAIMED LAND

Jack had heard some of the inmates in the ward say that unclaimed land was more readily acquired than many people might think. Small patches of stones on the side of a busy state route. Knolls of driving despair. Lost leases in a back hollow. Ravines of ill repute.

"String together a few, and you could have some acreage for the claiming," said a man in the ward, who believed that he always wore earplugs.

But these lands were fairy tales—products of wilderness minds. Unclaimed land in America was bullshit.

"More like Jack-shit," said Jack, as another landowner drove him away.

Jack pulled up his bed sheet. He stared at the ghost of Sid and hung his head.

"Where did that guy come from anyway?"

Jack stood in the middle of a chicken farmer's back

forty.

"Maybe you should try Sam Hill," said Merle Haggard.

The ghost of Sid drooled.

"There's gotta be something out there," said Jack, "besides tea."

Jack and Sid roamed the woods. It was high summer. They slept in small caves. They ate a few chanterelle mushrooms that smelled like apricots and drank boiled creek water with crushed spicebush. The tea crept in. Jack had no idea how to build a shelter or find more sustainable food. His bed in the Ford had been a plywood-induced feat of engineering. Finding the spicebush had been a happy accident that involved falling.

Then, Jack acquired the Pits.

ANDY WARHOL

Jack pulled the trigger.

"WHOOP!" said the gun. "Now I'm all dirty."

The gun was like that: finicky and particular. As a muzzleloader, it liked to be clean. The gun was also gay, but it had never told anyone that. The gun had been stored in a closet, where the darkness hid its scars. Perhaps the gun was the reincarnation of Andy Warhol.

Jack loaded another round of Pyrodex and lead with the short-starter and shoved the ramrod down the rifle barrel to seat the new charge.

The gun sighed.

The whitetail deer that Jack aimed to shoot had bounded fifty yards across the field after the black powder-induced explosion of missed opportunity. Standing in a patch of reprieved browse, the doe paused to look back at Jack. She stamped her foot three times. Then she stuck out her tongue and gave him the raspberries.

"Thpbpbpbpbpbpbp," said the doe.

She turned and quartered away to find her deer kin.

"Dammit," said Jack.

Jack had bought the inexpensive muzzleloader with idyllic thoughts to stave off his hunger. His thoughts encompassed a Virgilian pastoral set in the virgin forests of primitive America, where a white male hunter roamed free. These thoughts also represented his new locavore ethic: eat what you find and kill what you eat. The camouflaged redneck that sold the muzzleloader to Jack conveniently forgot to mention the pits.

"Yeah, that there's a real good firearm there," said the redneck, before his McDonald's-stained fist squeezed over the cash that Jack had earned selling scrap from the burned-out truck.

"You can have these, too," said the redneck, handing Jack a large quantity of sabot rounds, Pyrodex pellets, and the original manual that came with the rifle.

The redneck jumped into his monster truck and roared away.

His license plate read:

In reality, the muzzleloader was not a real good firearm. The redneck never cleaned the gun. The thought of cleaning the rifle passed through the redneck's mind once, as he sat drinking some High Power at his kitchen table, but then that thought drained away with the beer. The redneck had only fired the weapon fifteen times. He had used the sabot rounds that he had given to Jack—plastic-cup encased lead bullets that were made to seal the gas pressure in the firing chain of percussion cap to black powder to bullet launch bang. The sabot round traveled the length of the rifled bore, spun like a figure skater, and ejaculated from the muzzle, post-haste. The plastic wad was left spent upon the ground. The fertile round then hurtled off to points well sighted or largely unknown. Like all dirty acts, there was residue. The plastic-saboted projectile sealed in gas like a miracle of modern technological triumph over the old-style patch and ball, but this left a considerable build-up of plastic residue and Pyrodex by-product. Regular swabbing of the bore with clean cotton patches was necessary to keep the rifle accurate before eventual build-up required a thorough cleaning of the weapon. But the redneck didn't care about cleaning, swabbing, or any of that shit. He was used to firing a shotgun that didn't require much care. After seven shots with the muzzleloader, temperature and plastic began to conspire like an Alan Weisman nightmare. Shots went astray. By the redneck's fifteenth shot attempt sans swabbing, he said, "Fuck this shit," and he drank a beer. The redneck was convinced that the gun was junk. He was damned if he was going to clean the thing. The muzzleloader sat in his closet for a year, ashamed and unsure of what it was in the world. Its sanctimonious inner bore slowly oxidized. Moisture feasted upon its precious, but unclean, metal rifling.

It rusted.

The pits were born—small bumps and furrows of lost metal that wreaked havoc on the accuracy of the firearm.

After a year, the redneck sold the gun to Jack.

The redneck was scouting deer trails for the upcoming season when they met.

"Come on down out of that tree," said the redneck.

Jack sat on a tree limb above a deer trail with a large rock in his hand.

"I got a rifle at home might be a little better than that rock," said the redneck.

Now out of the closet, the rifle was rapturously free. Despite the pits, the gun loved Jack. Jack oiled the gun's barrel regularly, both inside and out.

After missing the deer, Jack and the gun headed back to the camp they currently called home. The ghost of Sid floated beside them.

"That shooting was the pits," said Jack. "Goddamn."

Jack and the gun were up early for some test firing the next morning. They were determined to find consistency; Jack was hungry. The ghost of Sid shimmered slightly in the cool mist of the morning.

Jack loaded the gay gun and fired away.

After sighting in the gun four times, shooting groups of three, Jack was still unable to group his shots. They weren't even close. He swabbed the bore with a piece of an old t-shirt. He began to question the gun. The muzzleloader had come from the redneck with an inexpensive, but functional scope, but it didn't help.

"Aren't these things supposed to be point and shoot?" said Jack.

The ghost of Sid sat nearby, panting and looking at Jack and the rifle. The ghost of Sid was not at all bothered by the fifty-caliber racket, or by the smoke from the rifle. The smoke reminded the ghost of Sid of the ghosts of bullets, and so he thought of the smoke as a friend. The ghost of Sid panted and smiled at his sulfur-smelling smoke-friends and thought of happy things and food.

Jack stared at the gun.

"I clean you," said Jack.

The gun didn't reply.

"I wash you," said Jack.

The gun squirmed in a metallic sort-of-way.

"What the hell?" said Jack.

The pits.

"This gun is the pits," said Jack.

The gay gun didn't like to be out of the closet now. It wished long wishes for the rusting safety of the darkness. It thought of all the good things about being in the closet and away from the hard truths of the world.

Jack eventually realized that his gun sucked. It was the pits. The redneck had pulled one off.

Jack didn't have any money to buy a new rifle. He had already salvaged all the Ford parts that he could move by hand.

"Okay," said Jack. "It's just me and you, Pits."

He swabbed away.

"And Sid."

The Pits was happy again. The Pits had meaning and a name. Though pitted, the Pits was out of the closet and ready for action.

"Goddamn," said Jack. "The Pits."

Jack and the Pits and the ghost of Sid headed back out to the woods to try to plug some deer.

They would just have to make due. Jack was used to that.

IN THE WOODS OF ARCHAEOLOGY

In the woods, Jack began to see the world anew. He found lithic tools with his newfound awareness. His empty stomach was an amazing motivator. Late Archaic points jumped into Jack's hands like groupies, as he scoured the terraced ridges above the Meandering River floodplain. He stumbled over rough-knapped chert. He fell into a three thousand-year-old fire pit and skinned his knees on ground stones and carbonized nutshell fragments. From that point on, everything in Jack's locavore world became subject to distant, fond, and shameful congenital memory. Jack was empowered, as he had never been before. To the maize-tinged darkness had come a bright white light: Jack had gone local. A worldly compassion for the earth and an indifference to the whims of the human race consumed him. He had taken in the Yellow. All was one. He was a walking, talking Gary Synder poem.

"Damn, I'm hungry," said Jack. "C'mon, Pits."

There were other cracks in the façade.

Jack couldn't identify any of the local trees. If asked by some ghostly figment of his imagination, perhaps the talking-ghost of Sid, to identify some twisting, bark-incrusted behemoth rising from an ancient burial mound or some smooth-skinned young sapling with the feel of glossy paper down by the creek's edge, Jack would invariably reply that it was one of the Seven Trees of Lucky Guesses: oak, maple, ash, hickory, walnut, pine, or dogwood.

The ghost of Sid appreciated that last one—dogwood.

"Potsherds!" yelled Jack.

A rumble vibrated the land.

The tremor was felt in a nearby cubicle at the state university, where dejected fieldwork teams of eager, young, shovel-wielding archaeologists sat reading textbooks, unearthing the grand, ancient art of grant writing.

"Did you feel that?" said Jack, to the ghost of Sid.

But the ghost of Sid didn't answer. He had popped out of existence.

Jack turned back to the tree before him. He needed a place to sleep. He had been driven from yet another property.

"I'm guessing this rotten oak tree would make a good house," said Jack.

The rotted-out sycamore tree was nearly four feet in diameter and sat close to a creek bed. It looked absolutely nothing like an oak tree, except that it was large when mature and that it was a tree. This sycamore, however, was long past mature and had entered into a phase of decrepitude that was only fitting for a locavore-idealist recently discharged from a state institution. The soft, spongy, yet resilient fibers of the sycamore wood had turned yellow and brown. A large opening at the base of the tree's trunk spilled forth in rotten splendor and allowed room inside for Jack and the ghost of Sid, who had reappeared, to sleep. The space was tight. Jack slept with his knees pulled up in a ball. The Pits sat propped up against the rotten wood beside his gallon of spicebush creek-water tea.

"Scoot over," said Jack.

The ghost of Sid shifted inside him.

THE REVOLUTIONARY

Ensconced in a shallow sandstone recess, the Revolutionary lit a hand-rolled cigarette and ran his hand through the fine sand that lay a foot deep on the floor of what passed for a cave around this part of the country. White quartz lucky stones stuck in the cracks of the Revolutionary's idealistic fingers as the fine sand sifted through and fell softly back into the dry sand. Spores of mildew, pigeon lice, and cave dandruff rose up to the Revolutionary's nostrils from the disturbance, like bourgeois prattle, and he thought of potato skin peelings falling into a cold childhood sink. His jungle boots pushed down into the damp underlayers of the packed sand.

An older model Fred Bear recurve bow lay on a sandstone outcropping beside the Revolutionary, heavily camouflaged. Red-crested arrows jutted from a homemade bow quiver attached to the bow.

The Revolutionary wore the requisite beard and military surplus fatigues of his ilk, and he carried a small, cheap, black-and-white journal to record any sudden flashes of communist insight that he knew might strike him at any moment, like Che Guevara lightning.

The Revolutionary picked up a yellowed gourd from the sand. He took a sip of strong yerba mate tea from the bombilla that protruded from the gourd. He ground his cigarette butt into the sand.

The Revolutionary listened to the bumbling approach of a man and his ghost dog.

"I hope it's not another one of those chicken farmers," said the Revolutionary.

A peculiar odor drifted downwind to the Revolutionary's nose. Sid, who sat drooling beside him in the sand, smelled it, too.

Sid's tail began to wag. It thumped in the sand like artillery fire and a plume of pigeon dandruff swirled into the air.

The Revolutionary stood up from the floor of the cave and grabbed his bow.

"Let's check it out," said the Revolutionary.

Sid ran to meet his ghost.

THE SUMMIT OF RED AND YELLOW

"Who the hell are you?" said Jack.

Fifteen yards away, a broadhead-tipped arrow patiently waited to enter Jack's incredulous heart. Behind the arrow, at full draw, was the Revolutionary. To Jack, he was a wild-looking, bearded man wearing mud-streaked face paint, a drab-green hat, military surplus fatigues, and a smattering of torn, Mossy Oak-brand camouflage clothing.

Only the Revolutionary's eyes were visible.

Sid smelled some leaves on the ground and peed on a pawpaw sapling. He had run up through the leaves and brush well ahead of the Revolutionary, certain that Jack was out there. When he reached him, he sniffed his pant legs and wagged his tail.

He couldn't help it; he was a dog.

Jack was confused.

"How'd you get so far ahead?" said Jack.

A moment before, he and the Pits and the ghost of Sid had been stalking a group of deer through the woods. Then, like double vision, Sid had come bounding through the leaves in front of him. The ghost of Sid had made a small *poofing* sound and instantly disappeared from Jack's side. Jack rubbed Sid's ears and said nice things to him.

"Good boy," said Jack.

"Good dog."

And, "Good old, Sid. Good boy."

It was the first time that Jack had petted the real Sid since the moment before his arrest. Jack didn't realize this as he stroked the dog's fur, although deep in his brain a tactile feeling was rekindled—synapses fired, neurons whirred. A vague notion of disparity lingered in his hand, and then the mud-splattered, arrow-wielding commando had appeared.

"What is to be done?" said the Revolutionary.

A small breeze came up from the south.

"Holla!" snorted a mother doe, catching scent of the humans and the dog and the Yellow.

The deer bounded off. The doe and her two deer children had been browsing thirty yards away when they heard the dog and felt the presence of Man. The deer were in a hollow and could not quite place the predators until the breeze gave away their position.

"Damn," said Jack.

The Revolutionary's arm was tired from holding back the fifty-five pounds of bow-drawn weight. He un-nocked his arrow and looked at Jack.

"You raise chickens?"

"No."

"I could use a cup of tea. Want to join me?"

Jack followed the Revolutionary back to the Revolutionary's cave like a flag. Sid trotted along beside them.

The ghost of Sid had vanished, but he would reappear each time the real Sid left Jack's presence, so that Jack was never without a Sid.

Jack and the Revolutionary sealed their friendship over tea. Jack moved his gear and his bed sheet into the cave the following day and, like the points on a compass, their lives took on direction.

Sid continued to sleep beside the Revolutionary.

Jack slept with the Pits at his side, and with the ghost of Sid, who was not nearly as warm.

UNLUCKY GUESS

"I wonder why that walnut tree doesn't have any walnuts," said Jack.

The Revolutionary looked Jack over.

"It'd be really nice to get some walnut meats sometime from that walnut tree."

"It's not a walnut tree," said the Revolutionary. "It's a locust."

"Locust?" said Jack. "Huh. I guessed for sure it was a walnut."

HIPPIE GIRL

Hippie Girl wore Birkenstock sandals, and her breasts bounced freely beneath the thin, gaily-colored dresses that she always wore. Her long, curly-blonde hair smelled of patchouli. She was pretty, but not overly so. Homely, but welcoming, was what Jack would later say, far down below in this narrative, like bones in the earth.

Hippie Girl preferred a different sort of tea: marijuana. She was in search of a hidden, sylvan glade for her special strain of dank weed when she met the Revolutionary. He was out practicing high-stepping parade marches interspersed with tai chi in front of his cave. Pin oak and redbud trees surrounded him like a vision of Joe McCarthy on mushrooms in a hallucinatory 1950's movie hall in America. It was an odd introduction.

Hippie Girl liked the Revolutionary's beard. His beard was a catalyst to free love. Socialism and hippie liberalism melded together in a left-wing congenital conspiracy of communion. They made love in the sand of the cave for hours, and they felt good. They were squatters-in-arms and passion burned in them like Molotov cocktails thrown at the Man.

Jack wasn't thrilled with the new arrangement. He drank his tea and took a long piss to think things over.

"I wish I was a ruminant," said Jack, to the ghost of Sid. "I'd drink one cup of tea and then several hours later I could re-drink the same cup of tea. Cud-tea. It'd save me a lot of time."

Hippie Girl moved into the cave. The cave was her home, not the highway.

"To each their own," said Merle Haggard.

"Right on," said Hippie Girl. "I'm glad to see that side of you."

"Just between the two of us," said Merle Haggard, "a working man has to pay the bills."

Together, Hippie Girl and the Revolutionary held a makeshift, illusionary red standard clenched in their fists. A peace-sign rainbow bloomed across the field of the flag, and a powerful red fist gripped it tight. The yellow fringe of the banner tinkled in the wind.

Jack found himself moved to the side. Free love did not yet extend to the Yellow. He was horny and jealous, but resigned to his golden state. He brewed another gallon of tea. At least, he still had the ghost of Sid.

"Good ole boy," said Jack, stroking the air where Sid was not.

The Revolutionary began teaching Hippie Girl how

to shoot his bow the next day. O, that smooth, archery action. It looked so good, it felt so right.

Str-

-etch.

Re-

-lease.

Thud.

"Cant the bow," said the Revolutionary.

It was awkward at first, but things settled down. Good things—harmony on the farm—rock it like Doc Boggs.

"He's pretty good," said Merle Haggard.

"Denizens of the Cave, unite!" cried Hippie Girl.

She was getting the hang of it.

She was Hippie Girl.

INTERLUDE: THE INTERNATIONALE

"The Internationale" has interrupted Merle Haggard. The anthem plays, stoic and lumbering. Merle Haggard and "The Internationale" hold hands uncomfortably, like secular and god-fearing hands praying together around the dinner table.

They echo in this sanctuary, like baptism.

Throats of heaven, in multiple octaves, embracing us all.

Horsehair strings their bows; animism controls their nature.

This is an interlude.

Thank you.

Merle Haggard will now resume, as a solemn fig leaf of beauty in the face of so much that should still be covered.

THE ROCKNROLLERS

Hippie Girl and the Revolutionary stared down at a group of local teenage rocknrollers. The rocknrollers stood beside their car smoking cigarettes, as the sun began to set behind the hills. The rocknrollers thought that they were alone. They had lit a small, shitty fire beside their car, so that they had somewhere to throw the butts of their cigarettes. Like a current of air rising in the morning, the Beatles' "Revolution" drifted up to the ridgeline from the rocknrollers' car stereo and into the socialist ears of the Revolutionary.

Merle Haggard was unperturbed.

The Revolutionary scratched his scraggly beard.

"The loneliest people out there are the musicians," said the Revolutionary. "They huddle around their squires like so many desperate roaches in the midst of jihad."

"Aw," said Hippie Girl.

"'Don't pick my worthless ass,'" said the Revolutionary. "'My friends pay to support this fiefdom and its ego.' 'We are outcasts.' 'I paid for this.'"

"Jeez," said Hippie Girl.

"The masses keep on massing," said the Revolutionary, "but their strongholds dwindle, except where Art retains its damaged grip."

The Revolutionary marched back into the woods. He had played in a band in high school, and it had broken his heart.

"That's too bad," said Merle Haggard.

"Right on," said Hippie Girl.

She didn't really care. She liked to dance. Her dances were all the things that spun around the THC-laden thoughts that clung to the inside of her skull, like brushing through cobwebs on a walk among the late summer trees.

Hippie Girl pushed through the dried weed stalks that bordered the oak woods and strode down the hill toward the rocknrollers in a lilting, half-stoned gait. Her Birkenstock-clad feet barely made a sound, although the gray, moisture-wicking socks that she wore squeaked ever so slightly against the leather grain of the sandals. She had an ounce of dope wedged down inside her dress between her breasts. The pot was in a plastic bag that Hippie Girl had found on the side of a road. The plastic made her sweaty and uncomfortable and threatened to slip down to her belly button. She had her sights set on the rocknrollers. Maybe she would bum a cigarette.

"Whoa," said the rocknrollers, as one, when they noticed Hippie Girl walking toward them, "a groupie."

The rocknrollers were uncomfortable, although they acted very cool. They were rocknrollers. They were cool.

"You guys want to party?"

"Uh, like, I don't know."

"What the hell."

"Yeah, like, we want to party. Yeah . . ."

"You guys like tea?" said Hippie Girl.

"For Texas?" said a rocknroller.

"This ain't Muskogee," said Merle Haggard.

"Merle, just be the backing track."

"Fine."

The insects voiced their word to the creepy-crawly world. The sun had gone down. The weathered, turtleback hills were dark all around them against the deep blue of the night sky.

"You wanna buy some weed?" asked Hippie Girl.

A rocknroller threw his cigarette butt into the shitty fire beside the car.

Hippie Girl spun a pirouette.

"You're not, like, the law or something, right?"

"Hell, yeah, that would be awesome."

The shitty fire the rocknrollers had burning burned.

It emitted some night light.

Hippie Girl took a drag off her mooched cigarette and pulled the plastic bag from her bosom.

"Let's rock," said the rocknrollers.

"Right on," said Hippie Girl, "but I gotta split. My old man's waiting for me."

Hippie Girl held the drug money tight in her hand until she had ascended the hill and waded back through the dried weeds of the ridgeline. She stopped and tucked the wad of ones down inside her sock, which was now covered in burrs. The nicotine from the cigarette rushed through her like blood. As she wound her way back through the trees to the cave, she thought about supermarkets and Jesus and about the price that we all pay.

The rocknrollers continued to burn strange woodstuffs that night for firewood. Cigarette butts were fun— also weed stocks and twisted roots. They made strange, beautiful forays into the surrounding woods for deadfall and scraps of burnable something.

"Let's burn my guitar!" said the ghost of rocknrollers past.

Held up to the Light.

PHONE CALL

"No. No, ma'am. We haven't felt anything here. Beetle Woods, huh? We'll send someone out to check on it. Thank you. Have a good day."

Ranger Four hung up the phone.

"Another one?" said Ranger Two.

"Yep," said Ranger Four, who now had a desk job after his run-in with Sid. "Said she felt a tremor when she was out hiking in Beetle Woods."

"I knew those fracking guys were lying to us."

"No shit."

"Probably drunk, too. I'll check it out. Never."

Ranger Two shuffled through a *Guns & Ammo* magazine.

"Hey, you ever hear anything about that mine monster?"

"Not much," said Ranger Four. "Few stories from old-timers."

"Hmm," said Ranger Two.

"Hey, wanna play some cards?"

"What?"

"Go Fish?"

"Sure," said Ranger Two. "I'm always ready to go fishin.'"

"Damn, that .356 looks sweet."

"Sure does," said Ranger Two. "Sure does."

IT

"We could try it."
Hippie Girl was baked.
"I'm up for it."
Jack was, too.
"Are you sure?"
"I'm an adventurous girl."
"I don't know."
"Why not?"
"So, have you seen it?"
"What?"
"Have you seen it?"
"Seen what?" asked Hippie Girl
"It," said Jack. "The Yellow."
"I will," said Hippie Girl.

HARRY NILSSON

"Far out," said Hippie Girl. "It kinda reminds me of *The Point!*"

"I'm not denying it," said Jack.

The Revolutionary was off in the forest with his bow, fiddling with his arrow.

THE WALLS OF THE CAVE

The Revolutionary walked up the slope to the cave.

"Where's Hippie Girl?"

Jack sipped his tea.

"I think she's down at the creek."

The Revolutionary made himself a cup of tea.

"Are you stoned?"

Jack was staring at the walls of the cave.

Merle Haggard echoed around them.

THE WOOD FAIRIES

"And what are these feats of vengeance that we wreak upon ourselves?" cried the Wood Fairies.

Jack glanced at the Revolutionary and hung his head over his cup of tea. Neither Jack nor the Revolutionary had been consulted on the Wood Fairies' move into the cave. Hippie Girl had simply come back from an evening walk through the woods and said, "Hey dudes, the Wood Fairies are moving in."

She held a glass jar in her hands.

"I found these guys out in the woods," said Hippie Girl.

The moonshine jar no longer contained moonshine, but it did contain the Wood Fairies. Hippie Girl placed the moonshine jar next to her dresses on a scavenged 2x6 piece of pine that served as her dresser in the cave.

"You reap because you sow!" screamed the Wood Fairies.

"What a bunch of existential bullshit," said Jack, who was still on edge.

"Shut the fuck up!" screeched the Wood Fairies.

The Wood Fairies were like white lightning at night, pulsating when everyone else wanted to sleep.

The Wood Fairies were also like the Napoleon complex of verbosity and all of them were named Tommy.

"It's like a fucking Greek chorus around here," said Jack, reaching out to pet Sid. Sid had dog-goop stuck in the corners of both of his eyes and a tumor growing on his belly. He looked at Jack and thought about chickens. He stood up after the requisite amount of petting and went back over to sit with the Revolutionary. The ghost of Sid immediately appeared in Sid's place beside Jack. Jack fingered away the ghost-goop particles from his ghost eyes and looked at the Wood Fairies.

"You shut the fuck up, Tommy," one Wood Fairy was saying to another Wood Fairy.

"Tommy, you don't know what the fuck you're talking about," said Tommy.

Tommy puffed up his wood fairy chest and unleashed another assault on the ears of the cave dwellers.

"Why did you invite these fairies in here anyway?" said Jack.

"I like fairies," said Hippie Girl. "Tommies, quiet down a bit and have some tea."

"I used to know a guy named Tommy," said Jack. "Wouldn't piss sitting down."

The Wood Fairies gave it a rest and drank their tea. The Wood Fairies drank a lot of tea. Early each morning, the fairies flitted from the holes punched in the lid of their moonshine jar and went about the woods collecting dew. The Wood Fairies only collected dew from one plant: poison ivy. Each Tommy had a special rag for collecting the dew. Once back in the cave, safe within their moonshine jar, the Wood Fairies wrung the dew from their dew rags and proclaimed it dew tea.

"The poison ivy gives it a little zing," said Tommy.

"Also, no one else will drink it," said Tommy.

"Fucking Tommy," said Tommy. "Always gotta get in another word."

"Jesus Christ, Tommy," said Tommy. "You've seen how much fucking tea that fucking guy drinks."

"Shut up and drink your fucking tea, Tommy," said Tommy.

The poison ivy tea didn't bother the Wood Fairies, except that it made them into even bigger assholes. The Wood Fairies had a natural resistance to urushiol, the volatile oil found in *Toxicodendron radicans*. They were also careful not to bruise the plants, as they extracted their non-lethal dew onto their little dew fairy rags.

"It's not really tea," said Jack.

"Vengeance!" cried the Wood Fairies.

"It's just dew," said Jack.

"May the poison bewitch your yellow pecker and turn you back into a man!" screamed the Wood Fairies.

"Poison tongues," said Jack. "Green, poison tongues."

Sid licked the Revolutionary's hand.

"Golden," said the Wood Tommies, "Just golden to the core."

"You guys are far out," said Hippie Girl.

The Revolutionary sipped from his bombilla. He was deep in thought. The Revolutionary was planning the next phase of his social revolution. Sid licked his hand again. The Revolutionary nuzzled his beard into the dog's face, and Sid smelled the small particles of delight stuck there like cannons bogged down in the mud. Sid rolled in the dirt on the floor of the cave and offered his tumorous belly up to the Revolutionary.

"Tommyknockers," said the Revolutionary.

TOMMYKNOCKERS

"May the oil lubricate your way to hell!" said the Wood Fairies. "May it seize up and spill your innards into the bowels of the Chasm! The Yellow Chasm!"

Hippie Girl puffed on her tea through paisley eyes.

Jack finished his cup of tea and readied himself for bed. He brewed another gallon of tea. He had heard enough of the Wood Fairies nightly diatribe.

Then they heard a silent knocking.

*

*

*

The Silent Ethiopian had come to call.

THE SILENT ETHIOPIAN

The Silent Ethiopian walked into the cave, but no one heard him. He was silent. The Silent Ethiopian stood six foot two and weighed one hundred and thirty-seven pounds. A leather pouch of teff flour hung from the Silent Ethiopian's belt, and another pouch of mint tea hung from the other side of his belt. A third pouch, made out of pleather, also hung from the Silent Ethiopian's belt, and this pouch contained sugar. The Silent Ethiopian would add some of the sugar to each cup of mint tea that he made for himself at each meal.

The Silent Ethiopian had made his two leather pouches out of an old baseball glove. After untying the lacing and cutting the leather, he pounded the rawhide with a round river stone for six hours. The baseball glove, which had once been loved, was old and tough. The Silent Ethiopian had found the baseball glove at a yard sale on a bright, sunny day. The glove lay on a table in a yard with too green grass beside an alarm clock, chintzy tableware, and a saltshaker with green, oxidized discoloration around its small shaker holes. The baseball glove looked like an old brown sandwich that had been left on the table much too long. The Silent Ethiopian bought that sandwich and cut it up and pounded away until he had two thin supple pouches, which he then filled with his teff flour and mint tea. There were no leftovers to make a third pouch. He tied all three pouches to his belt with the leather lacing from the baseball glove. As he chewed the laces to soften them up, the sweat of forty-one summers in America leaked onto his tongue.

Jack asked the Silent Ethiopian about the pleather pouch.

"Where did you get the pleather for that sugar pouch?" said Jack, after the Silent Ethiopian had lived with them in the cave for several days. "It looks funny beside the tobacco brown of your other two pouches."

But the Silent Ethiopian didn't answer.

He was silent.

This was well before Jack and the rest of the group had given up trying to make sense of the Silent Ethiopian and simply accepted him into their fold.

Under one ledge near the back of the cave, where crumbled sandstone sand reached helplessly up for sandstone rock, a seam of moist gray clay smiled a moist gray clay smile. The clay was gritty from the sand, but a small seep from deep within the rock kept it moist year-round. The Silent Ethiopian's slim dark fingers scraped the moist gray clay from beneath the ledge. He gathered the clay into plastic milk jugs that he borrowed from Jack, and soon he had a row of clay-filled milk jugs lined up next to each other along one side of the cave. The Silent Ethiopian was going to make a mogogo, the heavy clay plate used to cook injera, the spongy flatbread of his homeland.

A mogogo to cook his injera, an injera to still belong.

The Silent Ethiopian shaped the sand-grit clay and set about collecting wood. He needed a lot of wood. The mogogo was as inefficient as Jack's former tea-brewing operation by the Ford, but it was perfect for cooking his bread.

Jack helped the Silent Ethiopian drag armfuls of deadfall back to the cave. The ghost of Sid floated beside them.

"I wish I still had that dog harness," said Jack.

As the mogogo cured over a smoldering fire, volatile fumes arose from the clay and danced the tango with the pigeon dander floating through the cave.

"Gnarly," said Hippie Girl.

Jack drank his tea and watched.

The Revolutionary said, "There is no cure like a noxious cure."

The Silent Ethiopian mixed portions of teff flour and water in an opaque plastic milk jug and set it, loosely covered by a red cloth, against the rock wall of the cave.

The Silent Ethiopian left the mixture to ferment for three days. Bubbles arose like silent stories. Natural yeasts within the cave found the teff slurry and were overjoyed to suckle on a commercial product instead of the usual pigeon shit and dander. The yeasts felt liberated, as globalization could make one feel.

"Fucking traitors!" screamed the Wood Fairies.

After three days, the Silent Ethiopian stirred his bubbling sponge. He scooped out a small portion of the sponge and set it aside as a starter for his next batch of bread. He poured several cups of boiled Dead Orange Creek water into the remaining soured sponge.

The Silent Ethiopian dipped his cup into the batter. With a swirl of his wrist, the batter pooled onto the preheated mogogo and hundreds of story bubbles burst. The injera curled and browned on the edges. The Silent Ethiopian smiled a silent smile.

His work was good.

The Silent Ethiopian sipped his mint tea.

"Damn, that smells good," said Jack.

The Silent Ethiopian had joined the fray.

THE DEEP BREATHERS

The Deep Breathers sat in the leaves.

They looked up at the trees.

It was a windy day.

"The trees breathe," said the Deep Breathers.

"Like donuts," said the Deep Breathers.

"O," said the Deep Breathers.

The Deep Breathers were hiking in the woods and had stopped to rest as they began to climb a steep hill.

Below the Deep Breathers, walking through the sedge of an old clear-cut meadow, Jack and the rest of the cave dwellers were looking for something to eat.

The teff flour was long gone.

"Goddamn, I'm hungry," said Jack.

"We totally need to find some flowers to eat," said Hippie Girl. "I've got the munchies so bad I'm about to eat the stems."

"We need to find some mushrooms or nuts or something," said the Revolutionary.

"I miss the injera," said Jack.

The Silent Ethiopian was silent.

"'Shrooms," said Hippie Girl. "Right on."

"It's too bad the chicken farms have put up all those trail cameras," the Revolutionary was saying, as they left the meadow and stumbled upon the Deep Breathers sitting in the leaves.

The Deep Breathers continued to look up at the trees. The oak leaves crunched under them as they took in great breaths of air.

"Our lives are whole," said the Deep Breathers. "When we breathe, our lungs are like donuts."

"What the fuck?" said Jack.

"O," said the Deep Breathers, as the leaves crunched, and the wind blew, and the air filled their lungs like the hole of a glazed donut.

Everyone watched the Deep Breathers breathe.

Sid pointed at a bird.

"You might as well move into the cave," said the Revolutionary, whose chest had begun to rise and fall with the Deep Breathers' breathing.

"Wait till you meet the Wood Fairies," said Jack.

"Far out," said Hippie Girl.

The Revolutionary continued to focus on his breathing.

"A donut sounds really good," said Hippie Girl.

"Especially with some tea," said Jack.

The Deep Breathers stood up from the leaves.

Still hungry, they all walked back to the cave, breathing

as One.

"You guys don't have any, like, real food do you?" said Hippie Girl.

"O," said the Deep Breathers.

The Silent Ethiopian smiled.

The cave was getting crowded.

BEER CAN

Ranger Six kicked a beer can in the tall summer grass of the clearing.

"Nothing out here but a bunch of empty cans of Brush Lite," said Ranger Six, to himself.

He swatted at the swarm of mosquitos buzzing around his face.

Ranger Six was out in Beetle Woods. He walked back to his truck and called in to headquarters with his assessment of the situation.

"Nothing?" said Ranger Four. "We've had calls now for months."

"Well, I've been out here for hours," said Ranger Six. "Haven't seen a thing besides bugs. Plenty of beer cans, though."

"High Power?"

"Nah, just a bunch of Brush Lite mostly."

Ranger Six picked up one of the empty cans and set it on the rear wheel arch of an old Volkswagen Beetle.

"Okay," said Ranger Four. "Two's worried it might have something to with those old Locavore stories. Maybe an old mine giving out."

"Locavore? These local guys are crazy. It's the goddamn fracking is what it is. If anything. Besides maybe a bunch of drunk ass hikers."

"Yeah."

"And I didn't say that. About the fracking."

"Yeah," said Ranger Four. "You may as well head back in. Me and Two are gearing up for some Red Light, Green Light in the hallway. Come back in and we'll trade off on calling it."

"Sounds good," said Ranger Six. He crushed a beer can with his boot. "Hey, I got an idea. I'll bring some of these beer cans back and we can crush 'em onto our feet and play that way."

"Damn, I haven't done that since I was a kid," said Ranger Four. "That'll be fun as hell."

Ranger Six gathered up a twelve-pack of empty cans and tossed them into the back of his truck.

As he sped away, a tremor shook the ground. Acorns fell from oak trees. Birds lit from the branches of trees and shrubs. The empty can of Brush Lite toppled from the wheel arch of the Volkswagen and landed back in the tall grass.

FELLATIO

"People that perform fellatio are much less likely to get diseases," said Hippie Girl.

"Oh yeah, how do you know?"

"Well, only if you were born naturally," said Hippie Girl. "Otherwise, you don't get the right bugs to help."

"Oh," said Jack.

"The womb is a powerful thing," said Hippie Girl. "Rewarding, too."

The Revolutionary had left the cave with Sid to walk through the woods and think about revolution.

"This Yellow is the opposite," said Jack.

"Mm, maybe," said Hippie Girl. She paused. "But it seems powerful now."

"You're a miracle," said Jack.

"Miracles are magic," said Hippie Girl.

MOSQUITO NETTING

There were bats out and lightning bugs in abundance. The insects flew and danced in the clear night air. The humidity had dropped, but in the morning the sun was back out and hot. No one in the cave slept in a tent. They slept on the cool sand. Sleeping inside a tent would have meant early waking in the heat, as the morning sun shone down from the east into the shallow recess that they called a cave.

The Revolutionary did not like waking early. Waking early was the Revolutionary's Achilles heel in his long war against democracy and the sun.

"Bourgeois hours!" said the Revolutionary, when Hippie Girl said that they should sleep in a tent instead of on the floor of the cave.

"Then maybe we should find a cave that faces west?" said Hippie Girl. "We should think about our feng shui."

"It has to face east!" said the Revolutionary.

"I just don't get it," said Hippie Girl. "We need to, like, be here now."

"What's wrong with the floor of this cave?" said the Revolutionary. "Besides, it keeps you closer to the land."

"You say you want a revolution," said Hippie Girl.

The Revolutionary groaned.

"It just doesn't make that much sense," said Hippie Girl.

But the Revolutionary insisted.

The Wood Fairies flitted around the inside of their moonshine jar.

"Plus," said Wood Fairies, "you don't have any fucking tents!"

Jack rolled over on his bed sheet in the sand and covered his head with his arm.

The dog days of summer had arrived.

"Goddamn mosquitoes," said Jack.

His face was covered with welts.

The idea of mosquito netting flitted through the jungle of the Revolutionary's brain.

"Pennyroyal is the answer," said the Revolutionary. "Just make a concoction of pennyroyal, and the mosquitoes will buzz off like Americans when you mention the words 'socialism' or 'politics.'"

"I tried that once," said Jack. "Didn't help much with the Yellow."

"Shut the fuck up, Tommy!" said a Tommy.

Hippie Girl got up from the floor of the cave.

The Wood Fairies squeezed through the holes of their lid and flew off to collect their poison dew before the sun burned it away.

"Well, if you find some pennyroyal, find some food, too," said Hippie Girl. "I gotta go tend the weed."

The Deep Breathers had already walked into town. They sat on a sidewalk and watched a Pilates session through a soap-scrawled window three times every week.

The Revolutionary said, "I'm sure there was a time in our past when people were just like, 'If I could just sit down to shit, everything would be all right.'"

The Silent Ethiopian slept silently, close by his mogogo.

"It's starting to be more dark than light," said Jack.

The ghost of Sid was unrecognizable from the early morning fog.

Something was coming. Hippie Girl could feel it.

"Well, we're going to have to start getting some sleep soon," said Hippie Girl, as she left the cave.

"We need to find some goddamn food soon," said the Revolutionary.

Jack got up and began to make his breakfast: tea.

There was nothing in the cave to eat, unless you were a mosquito.

THE LOCAVORE

People in the town and the surrounding counties called it the Locavore, long before that name became synonymous with thirty-mile meal plans and yummy local vegetables. Myths and legends had grown up around the Locavore over time—a creature of the mines—something unearthed in the halcyon days of the coal mining boom and then bottled back up again before the terror was fully unleashed. For generations, county denizens had told ghost stories of the Locavore to their children at bedtime, as they sipped the last drops from their cans of Brush Lite.

"Watch out for the Locavore," the parents would whisper, in the darkness of their children's bedrooms. "Hope that it never finds its way out!"

The children would listen with wide eyes, surrounded by their plastic homes and the darkness that lurked all around them.

ACORNS

"You guys ever hear of the Locavore?" asked Hippie Girl.

Everyone was hiding from the sun in the cave, drinking or smoking their respective teas. They were all hungry.

"Yeah," said Jack. "Ghost stories. Nobody believes in ghosts." Jack reached down and scratched behind the ghost of Sid's ear.

"I heard the rocknrollers talking about it," said Hippie Girl. "Sounded pretty creepy."

"Tell me the story," said the Revolutionary.

Jack and Hippie Girl told the Revolutionary what they had heard about the creature that locals said was bottled up in a coal mine.

"My dad used to tell me that story," said Jack.

"Far out," said Hippie Girl.

"He was always drunk when he told it."

"We should call ourselves 'the Locavores,'" said the

Revolutionary. "We eat from the fat of the land."

"Right on," laughed Hippie Girl. "Groovy."

"I don't know," said the Wood Fairies. "Fairy tale creatures aren't always pretend."

The Deep Breathers sipped their chamomile tea.

"O," said the Deep Breathers.

"Today, we become the Locavores," said the Revolutionary.

Sid ran into the cave at the sound of the Revolutionary's voice. He had run off after a group of deer early that morning.

"We will draw from that power and use their stories against them," said the Revolutionary. "History will be written by change."

Sid's tail thumped in the sand.

The Silent Ethiopian scraped more of the clay from the seep under the ledge in the back of the cave and placed it in an empty plastic milk jug. The Revolutionary took the jug and began to paint the faces of everyone in the cave with the clay from the seep.

"With this war paint, we will change the world," said the Revolutionary. "It is a sacred bond that cannot be broken, but can be washed off."

The Revolutionary dabbed a spot of clay on Sid's nose.

"And it's totally good for your skin, too," said Hippie Girl.

"Tommy, you look like a fucking loser," said Tommy.

"Shut the fuck up!" screamed Tommy.

"I think you look beautiful," said Hippie Girl.

With their faces of clay, the Locavores danced around

the mogogo and inhaled its noxious vapors. They feasted on tea and a desiccated fast food hamburger that the Silent Ethiopian silently produced from one of his leather pouches. Then they were hungry for something more, something local.

"Anything else in there?" said Jack.

The Silent Ethiopian upturned the pouch. Nothing fell out but silence.

"We are the keepers of the code," said the Revolutionary. "We keep the old ways."

"Let us gather what nature provides," said Hippie Girl.

"Let us claim what the world has taken," said the Revolutionary.

"Let's get some chow," said Jack.

The newly christened and reinvigorated Locavores gathered as much food from the forest as they could find: bushels of recently fallen acorns, dubious late-season chicken of the woods mushrooms, a few decomposing pawpaws that no one liked, and several neon-lime-colored Osage orange monkey balls. They carried everything back to the cave in plastic milk jugs. Around the mogogo, the Locavores partook of their teas and feasted on the bounty of the land.

"Mmm, chicken," said the Revolutionary, as he bit into a very woody chicken of the woods mushroom.

The Silent Ethiopian gagged silently on a latex mouthful of Osage orange fruit.

Hippie Girl nibbled an underripe pawpaw.

"I feel like I just got done eating at that worker-owned restaurant in town," said Hippie Girl, as her stomach began to clench.

Jack smashed several acorns from their shells with a chunk of rock and ate them.

"I can't open my mouth," he mumbled.

"Fuck it," said the Revolutionary. "These mushrooms are weird."

The Locavores shit themselves for days.

The Silent Ethiopian shit silently into the weeds.

"Uh," said Jack.

The Locavores squirmed like grubs in the dander of the cave.

"We must re-learn the Old Ways," said the Revolutionary, as he ran from the cave again.

The ghost of Sid shimmered in the mist of the morning.

"We need to boil the acorns."

Hippie Girl retched and lit up a joint.

"We need to eat the seeds."

The Locavores were born.

DEER AND TEA

In the woods, the Revolutionary stalked. He had learned the maneuver. Countless hours of the feather. The twig. The slow walker. Moving in another plane.

Brush Knee maneuver, he thought.

The Revolutionary had recovered from his intestinal disruptions and was determined to bring some meat into camp.

Heel down. Stop. Listen.

The animals of the forest didn't recognize his presence. They were fooled by the dead hand of man.

The Revolutionary shot many deer, but they wouldn't die, at least not close enough by for the Revolutionary to recover them.

Injury. Pain. Suffering.

Death for no reason.

The wounded animals ran Somewhere Else to die.

Sid proved worthless at tracking them.

"Fucking asshole!" said a deer, lying gut-shot in the next county to the west.

It was hard for the Revolutionary to take.

His recovered arrows smelled terrible.

"Goddammit," said the Revolutionary, over and over again.

One morning, the Revolutionary finally put an arrow through the lungs of a young buck. He hadn't heard the Revolutionary creeping through the wet leaves after an overnight thunderstorm.

Flesh.

Meat.

The Revolutionary's heart thumped and cried, and he slit the manhood from the buck and opened the belly wide. The experience was both exhilarating and sad.

This was the world.

This you could not escape.

Sid enjoyed the offal, and the Locavores lived on, deer now themselves.

"Someday I'll get one with the Pits," said Jack.

Jack looked at the Pits.

The Pits looked back.

The Pits hung its gun-metal head.

"Maybe," said Jack.

BREAK

"Let's just give it a break," said Hippie Girl.

"Fuck," said Jack.

"I've just been feeling weird about it lately," said Hippie Girl.

"Or maybe you're just hungry?"

"Yeah," said Hippie Girl. "That and something else."

"Something else? The Yellow?"

"That shit is pretty weird, dude."

"Fuck," said Jack.

"Well, I told the Revolutionary anyway."

Jack felt cold.

"Chill, dude. He's fine with it," said Hippie Girl. "I think. He is a revolutionary."

Hippie Girl lit up a spliff.

"He got that deer," said Jack.

He took a drink of cold tea from a plastic milk jug.

"Whatever, man," said Hippie Girl. "Something else is going on, I can feel it."

"Something besides the Yellow?"

"Yeah, dude. Come on. It was fun, but I gotta deal with this shit. Plus, me and the Revolutionary are trying to make it work. You know how it is in that cave. We were just messing around."

Jack stared at the acorns around them. He took another drink of cold tea.

"Fine," said Jack.

Everything was Yellow.

Yellow sky.

Yellow birds.

Yellow trees.

Yellow bees.

"Let's finish our tea and get these acorns."

Jack and Hippie Girl and the ghost of Sid were close to Beetle Woods.

"There sure are a lot of acorns on the ground over here," said Hippie Girl, still trying to change the subject.

The ground vibrated and hundreds of acorns fell around them.

"What the fuck?" said Jack.

The ghost of Sid vanished.

Birds took to the air.

"Far out," said Hippie Girl. "I bet it's those fucking frackers."

The woods were quiet and still.

"Sure makes picking acorns a hell of a lot easier," said Jack. "Squirrels don't get them."

Jack and Hippie Girl looked at the acorns around them and at the woods where nothing moved.

"Where the fuck did Sid go?"

Hippie Girl looked at Jack.

Something was coming. She could feel it.

PEPPERS AND SKIN

"Peeling peppers is bullshit," said the Revolutionary. "The skin is the people's front."

Without a refrigerator, or salt, most the meat from the deer had spoiled within a week. It had dry aged into waste. Sid grew fat, but the Locavores grew hungry again. They didn't know how to dry the meat in the warmth of the yellow sun.

"This locavore shit is hard," said Hippie Girl. "Maybe we should try, like, gardening."

"Yeah!" said Jack. "Melons!"

"We must persevere," said the Revolutionary.

The Revolutionary sat on a large sandstone rock. He held a wrinkled, red sweet pepper in his hand. The issue with Jack and Hippie Girl had distracted him, but he had other things on his mind. More important things. The Revolutionary was trying to wrap his mind around his all-encompassing plan for social revolution.

"But I can grow, like, buff-ass weed," said Hippie Girl.

The Revolutionary stared at the sweet pepper. His plan had seemed so much more attainable not long ago.

"Seriously, man," said Hippie Girl.

"Be careful of enslaving yourself to their seeds," said the Revolutionary.

It was hard to think when he was always hungry.

"Whatever, dude," said Hippie Girl.

Before he met Jack, revolutionary ideas had flowed through the Revolutionary's brain like tea from a samovar. But now, boots in the sand, things had proven to be more difficult. Food was hard to find. Love was not always free. No one in the cave really knew what to do. The lessons of history were before them.

Fortunately for the Locavores, the Revolutionary had scored a boxful of sweet red pepper seconds that day from a local farm that could not sell red peppers with black holes and rotten insides to a discerning local public. The farmers had left the peppers in a cardboard box by the side of the road and gone home to drink some High Power. The Revolutionary spotted the peppers with his red eyes. He carried them back to the cave.

Everyone pitched in to carve out the rotten places. Jack helped the Silent Ethiopian roast the damaged peppers on the mogogo.

Thousands of seeds lay scattered on the sandy floor of the cave like miniature clams.

"Right on," said Hippie Girl. "At least we're having some peppers tonight."

She lit up some tea, and the silent sounds of Merle Haggard and the Silent Ethiopian echoed against the walls of the cave.

Soon, the peppers had all been roasted and cooled.

The Silent Ethiopian knew what to do; he would make a version of karya. He pounded the peppers into a paste sharp with too many skins, and the Locavores ate.

The Silent Ethiopian wished that he had made a fourth pouch for salt.

"Until you shit them out," said Jack.

"What?" said the Revolutionary.

"The skins."

The Revolutionary pulled on his beard.

"That's true," said the Revolutionary. "Undaunted, the people journey on."

CHAPULINES

"Let's make chapulines!" said Hippie Girl.

The tall grasses of autumn had begun to die.

The karya had not tided the Locavores over for long. They could only eat so many acorns. They were all hungry again.

Hippie Girl had eaten chapulines once at a hippie music festival that was held very far away from her current predicament of the cave. She had traded a back-to-the-earth food truck a dime bag of weed for them.

"Chappa-what?" said the Revolutionary.

"Chapulines."

Hippie Girl felt her body changing. She needed food.

"It's worth a try," said Jack.

"Let's do it," said Hippie Girl.

The Locavores ran through the tall grasses and through the dry fields.

Bandanas and dew rags flew like nets in an ocean of hope.

"Check out this grass," said Hippie Girl.

The brown grass was beautiful in the sunlight.

"Watch out, Tommy!" said Tommy, as a bandana narrowly missed him.

The Locavores dried their catch over the gentle, noxious heat of the mogogo. The grasshopper bodies dried into locally sourced protein.

"Weird," said Jack. "Tastes like popcorn."

"The masses will not starve tonight," said the Revolutionary.

"Gnarly," said Hippie Girl.

The Wood Fairies could not bear to watch.

Sid sat on the floor of the cave and dreamed of the lost taste of chicken. He gnawed on a thighbone from the deer.

But soon the grasshoppers grew too cold to jump. They forgot to put on their woolen mittens. Hunger grew in the Locavores like an inflating balloon.

"Let's boil some more acorns," said Jack.

"O," said the Deep Breathers.

Food was becoming scarce. The growing season was almost over.

THE OLD WAY

The Revolutionary called a meeting to order. He had a few ideas to impart on the Locavores. Hunger had begun to short-circuit his brain in ways not in line with social progress. The Locavores sat before him, crisscross applesauce, in a semi-circle on the floor of the cave. The Revolutionary smoked the last of his tobacco and told the others how it was.

"We have become like All," said the Revolutionary. "Our tongues betray us. Our tongues are the agents of Mother Culture. The words have been corrupted. The sounds have been coopted. The notes do not ring with the old sound. From this day forward, we will speak a new way. We will invent a new language. We will call it the Old Way. The words will be like leaves in the wind."

Jack drank his tea. He wondered if his tongue had turned yellow. He didn't have a mirror to check.

"But how do we form new words?"

"The Old Way consists of a lot of *ishes* and *ushes*."

"What's the word for baby?"

"Wish-wish," said the Revolutionary.

"And it will all come true," said Hippie Girl.

The Locavores began to speak the Old Way. None of it made any sense.

"What the fuck are you saying?" followed them around like the tail of a kite.

Sid became very confused, but he tried.

"Woo-sh woo-sh," he barked.

"O," said the Deep Breathers.

The Old Way was meaningless gibberish, but the Revolutionary insisted.

"Why do we have to talk this way?" said Jack. "We haven't gotten anything done in days."

"Ishish-tado-da-wish," said the Revolutionary.

"I don't know what you mean," said Jack.

"Wha-ish wa-oosh, ta-do-da wish," said the Revolutionary.

"I still don't get it," said Jack.

"The Silent Ethiopian hasn't had any problems!" screamed the Revolutionary, with revolutionary zeal.

The Silent Ethiopian stood silently against the cave wall.

"Fine," said Jack. "Ish-tish-tee-do de dee do dish."

"Wild," said Hippie Girl. "Ush."

The Locavores sat down to eat their bowls of boiled acorns, like squirrels in a foreign language film. The acorns tasted awful. The Locavores grew restless in the cave.

"Fuck it," said the Revolutionary.
"Thank god," said Jack.

MILK TICK

Milk Tick suckled at Hippie Girl's breast. Milk Tick was not born, so much as one day, Hippie Girl woke up and found her latched onto her swollen left nipple, like a parasitic, warm bun.

"Whoa," said Hippie Girl, "far out."

The Revolutionary had risen early and left the cave to go hunting.

"I think I'll call you Milk Tick," said Hippie Girl.

Milk Tick was focused.

"You're a miracle," said Hippie Girl.

Milk Tick looked at Hippie Girl, but did not break her latch.

"I love you," said Hippie Girl.

Milk Tick continued to suck milk.

"And what goes best with a warm bun," said Hippie Girl, "than milk?"

MILK TICK, PART TWO

"Where did she come from?" said the Revolutionary.

Hippie Girl didn't look up at him.

"She just showed up," said Hippie Girl. "Her name's Milk Tick."

Milk Tick was busy sucking milk.

"What the fuck?" said the Revolutionary.

MILK TICK, PART THREE

"I told you guys something was coming," said Hippie Girl.

"A baby?" said the Revolutionary.

"She's not a baby," said Hippie Girl. "She's Milk Tick."

The Revolutionary looked at Milk Tick.

She looked nothing like him.

"I don't get it," said the Revolutionary. "We've only been in this cave for a few months. You weren't pregnant."

Milk Tick swelled before them.

"It's a miracle," said Hippie Girl. "A miracle of the land."

Jack sat in the sand by the mogogo, on the other side of the cave, drinking his tea.

In Beetle Woods, the ground shook.

SUMAC

Hippie Girl grew tired of Dead Orange Creek water to wash down her chronic, dry-throated toking. Milk Tick was draining her. Hippie Girl needed new refreshment. There were no peppermint trees for the Locavores to pick peppermint candy.

"Good reference," said Merle Haggard.

"Huh," said Jack. "I never would have guessed that."

"Try sumac," said the Revolutionary.

"Isn't that poisonous?"

"No," said the Revolutionary. "Staghorn sumac."

The Revolutionary was nursing a bad case of buck fever.

"Just go get some sumac berries and make some lemonade. Do it before the rain, so that there's still some flavor."

"We can't find any food, but we can make lemonade?" said Jack.

"The berries are a deep red," said the Revolutionary. "Easy to spot."

"Righteous," said Hippie Girl.

The Deep Breathers breathed.

"O," said the Deep Breathers.

"Are you guys good for anything?" said Jack.

"O," said the Deep Breathers. "Donuts."

Jack was oiling the barrel of the Pits.

"Why don't you go buy us some goddamn donuts?" said Jack.

"If you do, I'll take a bear claw," said the Revolutionary.

The Wood Fairies rattled in the glass of their moonshine jar.

"I saw some sumac the other day down by the clearing along the bike path," said the Revolutionary. "Close to town."

The Revolutionary had taken to practicing his high-stepping parade marches on the smooth surface of the bike path, well away from the cave. Hippie Girl and Milk Tick had become a symbiotic pair. The Revolutionary needed space to formulate his master plan.

On the horizon, dark gray clouds rose like rain muffins in a baking tin.

Hippie Girl lit up a spliff and placed Milk Tick in a sling across her chest. She had made the sling from one of her paisley dresses.

"Let's do it," said Hippie Girl.

The Locavores left the cave and trooped down to the bike path. Years of creosote and herbicidal spraying had killed the will of many plants to live there, but not sumac. The sumac liked the shitty soil of the converted rail line. Clusters of sumac berries grew like small maroon Christmas trees at the ends of the sumac branches. Overhead, the cloud muffins had cooled and been upturned to rain.

"Let's get these berries," said Hippie Girl.

The Locavores cut the clusters of berries from the branches. They placed the berries in plastic bags that they collected from the bushes along the bike path. Soon, the plastic bags were as full as Santa's sack of toys.

The rain came down.

"I'll meet you back at the cave," said Jack.

The ghost of Sid floated after him.

The other Locavores returned to the cave. They blazed through cords of wood boiling Dead Orange Creek water over the mogogo.

Jack showed up a few hours later with an intact, neon-blue plastic trash barrel from the remains of the Ford. He dumped the sumac from the plastic bags into the barrel. As each batch of water came to a boil, Jack covered the berries with the boiling water.

"The stee-ping!" Jack sang again, falsetto.

"You should talk to the rocknrollers sometime," said Hippie Girl. "I heard they were looking for a new lead singer."

Merle Haggard said, "I prefer your baritone."

Hippie Girl smoked some pot and waited while the rest of the Locavores drank their teas. Milk Tick was latched onto Hippie Girl's breast.

Soon, Hippie Girl had sumac tea.

"What a great color," said the Revolutionary.

"It is like lemonade," said Hippie Girl. "But it's, like, red."

"Exactly," said the Revolutionary.

Hippie Girl now had eighteen and a half gallons of deep-red sumac tea. It was impossible to strain out all the bits of sumac berry detritus that floated in the barrel. The Locavores didn't have a chinois sieve.

"T-shirts work okay," said Jack.

"Nah, it's the natural way," said Hippie Girl, as she lit another spliff and drank her tea. "Unfiltered."

"Unfettered," said Jack, who was staring at her enlarged cleavage.

"Unbelievable," said the Wood Fairies.

"Shut the fuck up, Tommy," said Tommy.

Milk Tick suckled away.

Milk Tick preferred milk.

FLOSSITIS

One evening just before dusk, as the Locavores were eating their boiled acorns and feeling much more hungry than full, a bedraggled woman with a backpack stumbled into their cave. Sid, who was too hungry to really care, hadn't heard the woman approach until she was in the cave. He stood up, wagged his tail, and sniffed the woman's dangling hand.

"You don't look like a chicken farmer," said the Revolutionary.

"Huh?" said the woman.

"Want some acorns?"

The Revolutionary handed her a few acorns wrapped in a maple leaf.

The Locavores watched as the woman sat down and fumbled with the acorns.

The woman had little use of her middle or index fingers.

These fingers were blue. She had four blue fingers.

"What happened?" asked Jack.

"Flossing," said the woman. "I'm a dental hygienist. Chronic flossing."

Jack handed the woman a shelled acorn.

"Flossitis," said Hippie Girl, as Milk Tick switched sides.

The woman chewed the acorn for a moment before gagging and spitting it into the sand.

"Jesus," said the woman. She tried to dislodge a piece of acorn wedged in her teeth.

"Do I have anything in my teeth?" said the woman.

She dropped the leaf in the sand.

"You guys have any beer?"

"If you enjoy being sick, drink alcohol," said the Revolutionary. "Alcohol is the silence upon your soul."

"Especially tonight," said Merle Haggard.

"Hmm. Well, it's very important to take care of your mouth," said the hygienist, as she unslung her backpack. She pulled a can of High Power from the backpack and opened it with her pinkie.

"I don't see how you manage to keep working," said Jack.

"The beer helps," said the hygienist. "Plus, I'm covered."

Jack fingered the hem of the bed sheet from the Only Hospital Around.

The woman drank her beer.

Sid left the cave to find something to eat. And where the ghost of Sid should have appeared, the dental hygienist sat.

BLUE BALLS

The dental hygienist's name was Megan. She had been on a bender for several days. The dentist that Megan worked for hadn't been too happy with the way Megan's cleanings had been going lately.

"We can't have you flossing our clients teeth and then your own teeth at the same time," said the dentist. "Look at your hands. Your fingers are blue."

The dentist told Megan to take a week off to look after herself.

"Come back when you're ready to clean some teeth," said the dentist.

Megan bought three cases of High Power on her way home from the office and proceeded to get wasted between bouts of chronic flossing. She decided to go for a hike several mornings later to clear her head. She drank three High Powers for breakfast and loaded her a backpack with the remains of the last case.

Leaving beer cans like breadcrumbs that she would never find in her wake, Megan walked off into the woods. She set her backpack down after an hour in order to floss her teeth and that's when she realized her mistake. She had not packed her floss. Panic set in. Her fingers pulsed and the world suddenly had no direction. She looked around and there were only trees. She pulled some dried grass stems from the ground and ran them between her teeth. She drank another beer. Distraught and very drunk, she wandered through the woods all day looking for things to floss her teeth with until she smelled the noxious smoke from the mogogo.

She was soon on the doorstep of the Locavores' cave—alone, confused, and in need of a thorough dental cleaning. After their brief introduction and her last remaining can of High Power, Jack laid out a blanket beside his bed sheet. He and Megan curled up on the floor of the cave. Hippie Girl, Milk Tick, and the Revolutionary were already settled in across the cave. The Silent Ethiopian was silent.

"What the hell is this place?"

"We're the Locavores," said Jack.

"Those acorns were nasty," said Megan.

"Shut the fuck up!" screeched the Wood Fairies. "We're trying to get some sleep over here!"

The Deep Breathers were already catching some O's.

"Welcome to the revolution," said the Revolutionary.

"How do you floss your teeth?"

Milk Tick suckled on Hippie Girl, and the Revolutionary sipped from his bombilla, as night closed around them.

"Want some tea?" asked Jack. He had a full jug ready for the night beside him.

"No way," said Megan. "Never touch the stuff. It stains your teeth. Got any Brush Lite?"

Jack grew uncomfortable on his disgusting sheet.

"Want to fool around?" the dental hygienist whispered.

"I think you're still wasted," said Jack.

The fire of the mogogo dimmed and released more noxious vapors, like cancerous bunnies jumping from a clay hat.

The hygienist snuggled closer to Jack.

Hippie Girl didn't mind.

She had Milk Tick.

The Revolutionary was warm beside her.

She was also very stoned.

Jack and Megan began to mix colors.

"What's that?"

"Well," said Jack.

Unable to properly make use of her hands, Megan pushed herself off the blanket on the stumps of her elbows and ran from the cave.

"So much for green," said Hippie Girl.

She lit up a roach in the darkness.

The poisonous bunny vapors copulated in the night air of the cave.

The ghost of Sid rolled on the blanket beside the spurned and prostrate body of Jack.

"More like blue balls," said the Wood Fairies, who never showed an ounce of empathy inside their moonshine jar.

"Fucking blue balls," said Tommy.

"Fucking blue balls," repeated Tommy.

Jack rolled over and stroked the ghost of Sid.

"Goddamn Yellow," he said.

But Megan came back. She didn't know how far she was from town, and the night was cool. She took the blanket that Jack had laid out for her and moved it over close to the mogogo. The blanket passed through the ghost of Sid like Sawing a Dog in Half before Jack's incredulous eyes. Megan began to sleep beside the mogogo every night. And whether or not she began to sleep with the Silent Ethiopian or not, no one could say. The light from the mogogo was dim, and the Silent Ethiopian never spoke a word to anyone.

"I kinda like it here," said Megan, as she flossed her teeth before bedtime with some dried blades of grass.

Her fingertips swelled and turned deeper blue, and then purple, from the pressure of the grass twisted tightly around her fingers.

"But it's too bad there isn't any High Power."

SLEEP

Jack lay asleep with the ghost of Sid beside him. The Pits was propped up against a recess in the cave wall. A children's bicycle leaned precariously on its kickstand in the sand near Jack's head. For a moment, the tassels on the handlebars vibrated in the night air. Something had begun to lurk in Jack's dreams, shining like a golden rod in a field of darkness.

THE KLAN

The wheels of Jack's bicycle popped over the acorns that lay on the dirt path before him.

Jack had found the bicycle a few weeks before Megan's arrival at the cave, when the heat of summer and the days of grade school vacation had come abruptly to an end. Like college students living in a throwaway culture, the local kids had taken to ditching their bicycles against trees, in gutters, sometimes in the middle of the road, and especially in front of their parents' homes. They left the bicycles to rust where they fell. The pink, white, and blue tassels on the handlebars of the bicycles flapped in the early autumn wind.

"Daddy will buy me another one," said a little girl.

"Fuck it," said a little boy.

"Don't say 'fuck,'" said the little boy's little brother.

"Get ready for school."

"I don't like that color anyway," said the little girl, who like the rest of the children had spent the majority of the summer inside her house playing video games.

"Come on inside, kids!" yelled their mother. "I've got some Brush N/A for you!"

"Yay!" screamed the children, readying themselves for a life in the town.

Jack had found one of these bicycles covered in leaves along a dirt path, like a relic of an autumnal Pompeii.

Jack threw his acorns down, blew off the leaves, and climbed on. The ghost of Sid fluttered behind him for days afterward as Jack pedaled on the paths through the woods. The backs of his elbows became sore from his knees smashing into them. At every turn, Jack attempted to outrun the Yellow, which clung to him like a Post-it note stuck to his front.

One afternoon, as Jack rode through the autumn woods on a ridgeline path cut by dog walkers, he heard the low voices of a congregation. Jack slowed the bicycle and set it against a tree.

"Not again," said the bicycle, which had already had its fill of abandonment.

Jack lay down on his belly and scooted forward on his elbows as if he were stalking a group of deer just on the other side of nowhere.

"Hey, you can't use that."

"Shut up, Merle Haggard. Just go back to being the backing track."

"But that's a Kris Kristofferson lyric. He's a friend of mine."

"I know, but it sounds poetic, and it fits the situation. Besides, it's a good tip of the hat."

"A two-fer."

"Yeah."

"Fine. But you should respect the artist."

"I do, I do. Now just let me get back to this."

Jack pushed himself up against a shagbark hickory tree and peered down into the hollow from which the voices arose like a poorly executed Gregorian chant.

In the hollow, a congregation of white-robed figures stood in a ragged circle wearing white-pointed hats.

"What the fuck?" said Jack. "The Klan?"

Below, the voices were speaking, but Jack couldn't make out the words in the largeness of the woods. Above him in the hickory tree, a squirrel had begun its croaking litany of trespassing. A deer would have heard the squirrel and heeded its warning, but the group wearing the white bed sheets had other things in mind. Their meeting was just breaking up, and they were ready to disrobe.

"Think we fooled anyone?" said Regnar Xis, one of the white-robed congregation.

"No," said the Ffirehs.

"Might have," said a Namwal.

The group had just returned from a torch-filled jaunt through the streets of the town.

"I can't wait till next Thursday," said Regnar Owt.

"I saw a few freewheeling drifters downtown that might want to play," said the Namwal.

"Might as well dig a hole or three here," said the Ffirehs. "Good a place as any."

The Ffirehs took off the white hat that covered his head.

"Time to get back to the wife," said the Sheriff. "Said she was makin' chili tonight."

"I think this might be close to where they buried the Locavore," said Ranger One, as the congregation all took off their white hats and sheets.

"Nah, I heard that was over in Beetle Woods," said Ranger Two.

"Don't tell my kids," said a Lawman.

"You guys ever feel the ground shaking out there?"

"Well, if you did, it's probably from the fracking."

"Yeah, well, some no-good drifters are gonna be sleeping with that monster soon no matter where it might be," said the Sheriff. "And you boys will be feeling the wrath of the Australian continent."

"No, no, Sheriff," said Ranger Two. "Gonna be a night for South America."

The group guffawed and grew misty-eyed at the prospect of another night of moving plastic pieces across a game board in the quest for world domination and the bludgeoning of another poor fool that believed that the game of Risk was only a game and not his last night alive on this earth.

Jack crawled back away from the hickory tree and grabbed his bicycle.

"Those fucking walnut trees are scratchy," said Jack.

The squirrel watched him go.

Jack sped through the acorns and the hard clay dirt and the fallen twigs that could still puncture the wide tire of a kid's bike. The tires slalomed along the packed clay ridges into wet mud, and then leaves, and down hills, and eventually all the way back to the Locavores' cave.

Jack set the kickstand on the bicycle and made a cup of tea. He placed those white robes into a deep pocket of his mind. The contents of the pocket were layered by time. The loony bin was close to the surface, but those white robes were closer to weird.

The Yellow remained, as always, on top.

STORAGE COOKIES

"Do you know where the storage keys are?" asked Hippie Girl.

"No, why?"

"I need to store these cookies."

"You're storing cookies?"

"Yeah," said Hippie Girl. "Storage cookies."

"But this is a cave."

"Right," said Hippie Girl.

Beside them, the Silent Ethiopian was silent.

"On," said Hippie Girl.

Milk Tick said, "Nah."

That meant nurse.

Milk Tick had begun to say that a lot.

"Nah," said Milk Tick. "Nah. Nah. Nah. Peas."

Peas meant please.

Milk Tick had no need for round green vegetables.

Milk Tick needed milk.
"Nah. Peas."

TAI CHI

The Revolutionary began.

"Every time he begins to do tai chi," said Jack, "you know he's had too much tea."

The Revolutionary heard Jack and focused.

It began to go all over, even though it was supposed to be right there, but he had this under control.

Things are slightly wrong. But fine—focus.

"You're starting to be like this all the time," said Jack.

The Revolutionary went into further complex, fibrous movements of slow motion. He bent this way. He bent that way. He crouched down very low in the sand of the cave and got the butt of his fatigues even dirtier than they were before the tai chi started.

"O," said the Deep Breathers, completely satisfied.

Hippie Girl returned to the cave from tending her crop.

"What's the Revolutionary been drinking?" asked

Hippie Girl.

Milk Tick suckled at her breast.

"Too much chai tea," said Jack.

The Revolutionary was out of yerba mate.

"That doesn't seem too local to me," mouth-farted the Wood Fairies.

The Revolutionary focused on his movement. He recalled his successful stalk on the deer—that rare victory in their campaign against hunger.

"I could sure use a High Power," said Megan.

Jack drank his spicebush tea. It had been a long time since he had tasted beer.

"Actually, I could use a case of High Power," said Megan. "A case would be great."

Hippie Girl had traded a quarter of dank weed for the chai tea. The rocknrollers had not been able to come up with enough money to pay for their weed.

"We thought we would make more money at the show," said a rocknroller. "But they only gave us, like, twelve dollars and some High Power."

"I don't want any beer," said Hippie Girl. "I've got high power."

"Oh, we drank that at the show, anyway," said the rocknroller.

"We have some chai tea," said the new singer of the band, who had a sore throat from singing.

"Yeah?"

"And some future drugs," said the singer.

"Hmm," said Hippie Girl. "Whatever."

Back inside the cave, the Revolutionary twisted in slow,

arcing circles. He had drunk all the chai tea himself, as if the tea were a packet of cyanide on the eve of the Party's destruction.

"No one else likes that kind anyway," said Jack, as the Revolutionary went at it.

Now, the Revolutionary was hopped up on chai tea and had commenced the tai chi. The Revolutionary Carried the Tiger Over the Mountain.

"Repulse Monkey!" shrieked the Wood Fairies. "Repulse the fucking Monkey!"

The Silent Ethiopian burped silently beside the mogogo.

Hippie Girl took a deep puff from her joint and watched the Snake Creep Through the Grass. She fondled the packet of future drugs hidden in her dress.

Maybe I'll try them tomorrow, she thought.

The Revolutionary focused on his plan.

In the future, thought Hippie Girl.

THE GROCERY STORE

The Locavores invaded the grocery store, like commandos in the daylight hours. Sid waited outside.

"It's time to execute," yelled the Revolutionary.

The grocery store was a chain supermarket with plenty of non-local products: all of them.

The Locavores quickly fanned out.

The Revolutionary unfurled their t-shirt banner and planted it in the produce section, supported by branches from the ornamental crabapple trees outside in the parking lot:

"It's a good thing those little maple trees were growing outside," said Jack, who had been responsible for bringing the branches for the banner.

The Revolutionary pulled a length of chain from Megan's backpack. While he chained himself to the non-organic avocado bin, Jack and the Silent Ethiopian erected a tall pole in the center of fifty-two plastic packages of green beans. The Silent Ethiopian had fashioned the pole out of a young cottonwood tree.

"Beautiful," said Jack, admiring the work. "Oak, huh?"

The Silent Ethiopian grabbed a roll of produce bags next to an apple display and ascended to the top of the pole. He was not wearing any shoes and should not have been allowed into the store at all.

"Mommy, that man's not wearing any shoes," said a little girl, in a pink plastic kid cart in the shape of a car.

"No, honey, we don't need any green beans," said her mother. "Just some Brush Lite."

The pink cart was unwieldy. The girl's mother could only move it by keeping her head down and pushing it with all her strength. She pushed the cart past the green beans and up to the avocado bin. An avocado lay on the tile floor, dislodged by the chains of the Revolutionary. The mother bore down and squashed it into guacamole.

"I'm a patriot of ideas, not institutions," said the Revolutionary.

The Silent Ethiopian strapped himself to the cottonwood pole with the plastic produce bags. He looked like Jesus

Christ crucified above green beans.

With the Silent Ethiopian and the Revolutionary garrisoned within the produce, Hippie Girl began to throw handmade Locavore pamphlets ridiculing non-local foods across the produce bins, as if the pamphlets were non-GMO corn pollen spreading across the aisles of our modern foodways.

Jack couldn't decide where he should chain himself. He had planned on finding the tea aisle, but the others had coalesced around the produce like moths on cabbage. Jack picked up the backpack and took out another length of chain. He wrapped the chain around a bin of lemons and black garlic.

"Black fucking garlic," said Jack, ignoring the lemons.

Megan was also not were she hoped to be. She stood next to a bin of partially husked sweet corn. The ears of corn reminded her of flossing, and her blue fingertips pulsed like need. She couldn't use her hands well enough to secure herself to the bin, so she just sat down beside it.

As soon as these fuckers look away, I'm making a break for Oral Care, she thought. *Maybe grab some High Power, too.*

The grocery store had a full working bakery that produced various breads, donuts, cakes, and pastries from ingredients shipped in from Somewhere Else.

"Doesn't that make it local?" said Jack, reading the signs. "If it's made here?"

"Faux-local!" yelled Hippie Girl.

The Deep Breathers breathed. They had wandered over to the pastry display. Inside the glass case, rows of glazed donuts sat in the lotus position on waxed paper.

"O," said the Deep Breathers.

"O," reverberated the donuts.

Behind the counter in the bakery's ovens, loaves of bread expanded like lungs filling with air.

The Revolutionary shook his chains.

"The continuity of foodways," said the Revolutionary, "that is the key to cooking. The lessons learned until the flow replaces hungry and the need to provide becomes primal."

"A pound of ham, please. Sliced thin," said a customer, at the deli counter, which was close to the produce.

"Humans discovered consciousness in hot climes. Their guilt over wasteful eating and killing led to the ways of preservation."

"Get stoned, not stupid!" yelled Hippie Girl.

"Where the fuck are the Wood Fairies?" screamed Jack, right when he needed them most.

Near the front entrance, the ghost of Sid floated through a rack of Halloween candy.

The Locavores all wore white t-shirts that they had decorated on both sides:

They also wore bandanas, like outlaws, across their hungry mouths. Hippie Girl had tie-dyed her t-shirt and Milk Tick's improvised onesie with her sumac-lemonade. Peace signs, flowers, and a primitive replication of a goddess of fertility adorned both of their shirts as well.

The Deep Breathers had stolen the t-shirts from a sidewalk display after their last Pilates-watching session in the town.

"Did you get something to write with?" said the Revolutionary, while the Locavores were still in the cave. "I only have a pencil."

"O," said the Deep Breathers, "no."

"We need some paint," said the Revolutionary. "Something to write with."

"I've still got Sharpie," said Jack, pulling the marker from his pants.

"More like 'Nasty,'" said the Revolutionary.

Back in the produce section, no one cared.

"Those are some nice green beans," said an old lady, moving aside the dangling feet of the Silent Ethiopian.

"Get some potatoes."

"Oh, excuse me, young man."

The old lady bought two packages from the Golgotha of green beans. The green beans were sprayed with toxic sludge, but she didn't care. The beans would taste nice with the potatoes and a smoked ham hock pumped full of industrial waste products.

She already had cancer anyway. Almost everyone did— lurking in their cells like the Yellow.

"Hey, look," said Hippie Girl, "it's the rocknrollers."

The rocknrollers were stoned. They wandered the aisles of the supermarket with halo eyes. They were on a quest for tzatziki sauce.

"Where the hell is the tzatziki sauce again?" said a rocknroller.

"Maybe we could just make some," said a different rocknroller.

"We can't make it if we don't know what it is," said the singer of the band.

The Revolutionary continued his proselytizing.

"You've just forgotten. People have just forgotten how to live. People that just go out and buy their food," said the Revolutionary, "they have just forgotten how to live."

Around the Revolutionary, grocery store patrons chose close bunches of bananas, exotic dragon fruits, and vegetables that they believed in.

"Some people," said Hippie Girl, to Milk Tick, "just do not want to be part of the show. It's your job not to make them part of the show. Don't. Just do your job. Entertain them and carry on like you are conducting the show, which you probably aren't if you are thinking about it."

"Yeah," said Jack. "Pony up some cake."

The Wood Fairies rounded the end of an aisle with a large assortment of boxed tea.

"Let's get the fuck out of here!" shrieked the Wood Fairies.

"Good idea, Tommy!" screamed Tommy.

"Tommy, look at those fucking kumquats!" said Tommy.

"Grab the fucking tea, Tommy!" said Tommy.

"Tommy! Fucking jackfruit! Holy fucking shit! Did you see this, Tommy? Jackfruit!"

Boxes of tea spilled onto the guacamole floor of the grocery store.

Alarm bells began to ring.

The manager of the grocery store was pissed.

"Law's on its way!" the manager said, over the store's intercom, briefly interrupting the food-shopping top forty soundtrack.

"We got some chai!" yelled the Wood Fairies.

The Revolutionary threw off his chains.

"Jack, is that you?" said Hippie Girl.

One yellow banana lay in the banana bin. Some asshole had pulled one banana from a bunch and left it there, alone.

Hippie Girl picked the banana up and waved it in front of Milk Tick's face.

"Stick that thing in your holster," said the Revolutionary, "and help me get Jack."

The Silent Ethiopian slipped down from his cross and left the store without a sound. Plastic produce bags multiplied across the floor like fishes and loaves.

The Revolutionary was having troubling extracting Jack from the black garlic and lemon bin.

"Excuse me," said a woman, who needed a lemon.

"The revolutionaries are the true souls," said the Revolutionary. "The pure beings. The ones who look at the skies, who look at the ground, and see beyond itself to itself. They are a dying breed. But they will always be around—sometimes, less strong than before."

"Let's go," said Hippie Girl. "I'm, like, wasted."

The Locavores left the grocery store.

"Hey, let's grab some of those tortilla chips," said Hippie Girl, as they passed by the dumpster behind the grocery store.

The Law showed up late.

The cottonwood pole still stood like a cross on a hill of green beans.

"In the green beans, huh?" said the Lawman.

"Yep, in the green beans," said the grocery store manager.

"Dangerous game," said the Lawman.

Overhead, the top forty played like the need for milk.

VW PINCUSHION

Jack and the Revolutionary rode imaginary horses through the woods, over greenbriers, and across a half dozen sandstone outcroppings to Beetle Woods. Jack had left his bicycle behind, but the Pits was in his grip. The Revolutionary's bow was at the ready. Their target was a 1967 Volkswagen Beetle. The front hood of the light-blue Bug lay buried in the ground, as if attempting to dig itself back into some vehicular burrow. Or maybe it was a wormhole to the Summer of Love, far away from its Appalachian predicament of a land that time forgot. Whatever the case, the Beetle was well documented in the local Coleopterist Society for Tourism. Countless brochures advertised this section of woods and the partially entombed car that protruded at a thirty-degree angle from the earth.

Locals would reference the car as well when they were deciding where to spend their time in Wang National.

"So, where you wanna hike this weekend?" an aging mother might ask her indigent son.

"Beetle Woods?"

"I'll get some High Power."

"Nah, make it Brush Lite."

Once Jack and the Revolutionary arrived at the Beetle, the Revolutionary's green two-bladed arrowheads zipped through the air from his Kodiak Magnum recurve and pierced the Beetle's side door.

"¡Viva la revolución!" yelled the Revolutionary.

The cold sound of metal on metal rung out across the subsidence of the land. Many of the wood-shafted arrows broke upon impact, leaving only expensive Port Orford cedar-shafts stuck in the faded metallic hide of the Bug.

The Revolutionary hated cars. He had been in car wreck several years before, and people had died. Since the wreck, his brain had not stopped crossing the ping-pong table of the accident. Cars, for him, had come to symbolize both the fragility and the incompetence of humankind. The next phase of the Revolutionary's revolution had begun.

The Revolutionary picked up one of the broken cedar shafts and held it to his nose.

"I love that smell," said the Revolutionary.

The ghost of Sid hovered beside one of the round metal hubcaps of the Beetle and peed as high up on the tire as his ghost-pee would reach.

"Get out of the way," said Jack.

Jack took aim.

"WHOOP!" said the Pits.

Jack squinted through the Pryodex-laden air. He had

no idea if his shot had struck its mark. He couldn't see a thing through the smoke. He galloped to an imaginary stop and reloaded one hundred grains of Pyrodex and a lead round, and rammed them home.

"WHOOP!" said the Pits.

The backside windowpane of the VW exploded.

The Pits was overjoyed.

"Swab me!" said the Pits.

Every hiker in the vicinity heard the shots, but no one paid much attention to them. A few tourists headed back to their cars. Shooting a local landmark full of holes might draw the ire of a few conservationists, or the Rangers, but not many locals. Deer season was approaching. People had to practice. Most of the locals were too drunk to care anyway.

The locals prayed to a High Power.

"Kill the Bug!" Jack screamed.

"I shouldn't have used my Zwickey's," said the Revolutionary.

"That Bug is extinct," said Jack.

He looked at the Pits with a newfound love.

Far below the surface of the earth, but well in line with the Beetle's trajectory, a tremor of sound vibrated up and into the ears of the ghost of Sid.

The monster stirred.

Jack noticed.

"Did you feel that?"

"Feel what?"

"Sid noticed."

"We left Sid at the cave," said the Revolutionary. "You

know he's scared of the gun."

Jack looked around.

The ghost of Sid had vanished.

"Weird," said Jack.

"These points aren't coming out of this metal hide," said the Revolutionary.

His store-bought supplies dwindled.

"Sid sure doesn't like that fracking," said Jack.

The car killers continued their campaign in the weeks to come, hell-bent on motorized destruction. On their imaginary horses, they rode up to unoccupied and broken-down cars and trucks and shot them down like bison. The Revolutionary switched over to handmade reed arrow shafts and rough-knapped chert points—many of which Jack had found. Megan's blue fingers proved deft at tying the points and fletching.

"I'm pretty damn hungry, though," said Jack, after they had filled a Buick full of holes. "Maybe we should try to get another deer, instead."

Jack's Pyrodex supply grew ever closer to none.

He looked at the smoking barrel of the Pits.

"Let's ride," said the Revolutionary.

Jack and the Revolutionary rode off into the cave, and the ghost of Sid, who had returned, trailed not far behind.

CAVE BATHING

"The Europeans were right," said the Revolutionary.

He lay on the floor of the cave, suffering from an insufficient amount of caloric intake. He and Jack had just returned from their latest attack on an old Demolition Derby station wagon. The station wagon sat in the neglected field of a chicken farmer like a devastated monument to the number eighty-eight.

"Oh yeah?" said Jack. "About what?"

Jack was sucking on a white quartz lucky stone to stave of his hunger and thirst. Dead Orange Creek had run dry.

"Bathing," said the Revolutionary.

"How so?"

"It's a good idea not to bathe very often," said the Revolutionary, scratching at his armpit. "Although it's uncomfortable at first, the bacteria need to find a natural rhythm."

"You've been talking to Hippie Girl about this haven't you?" said Jack.

"The bacteria protect you like fermentation."

"Skin fermentation?"

"You'll see," said the Revolutionary.

The Revolutionary looked forward to the future.

Everyone in the cave looked forward to the future.

A future with more food.

Hippie Girl and Milk Tick were taking a nap beside the Revolutionary.

Jack asked the Silent Ethiopian what traditional Ethiopians did about washing themselves, but the Silent Ethiopian didn't have anything to say concerning the grooming habits of Sub-Saharan Africans.

Sid panted away at the Revolutionary's side, freaking out every time he heard the word 'bath.'

"I think I'm going to go to the waterfall the next time it rains," said Jack. "No more cave bathing."

"If you find any acorns, bring some back," said the Revolutionary.

"A case of beer would be good, too," said Megan, who was flossing her teeth with a dried stem.

The Revolutionary rolled in the sand on the floor of the cave like a dust caterpillar. He was filthy.

"Make sure you try to find some acorns," said the Revolutionary, "when you go."

TOURIST FALLS

A tourist fell from the cliff above the waterfall. The fall from the cliff was a long one and usually fatal. Sometimes, a tourist might survive to live as a cracked vegetable in a white room for a time, but not usually. Tourist after tourist plunged from the sandstone cliff above the waterfall.

Thud.

It had finally rained.

Jack waded into the cold water that formed a shallow pool below the waterfall.

Here comes another one.

Tourists and locals had been visiting this waterfall for over a century. Many had left their names etched into the sandstone of the cave with their penknives. Native peoples had used this recess for shelter, but they had not written:

JOHN
1901

People visited Tourist Falls to see the beautiful waterfall, and the pretty cave, and the scenic view, and for the chance to step outside of their electronic lives.

"Oh, what a beautiful waterfall," said a wife.

"Oh, what a beautiful cave," said a husband.

"Ahhhhhhh," said a male tourist, as he fell from the cliff and shattered in the shallow pool of the waterfall.

It wasn't a good place to get clean, but people enjoyed wading there.

Jack scrubbed at his armpit with a scrap of t-shirt. He had stripped down to a pair of cut-off shorts. The water was very cold. As soon as the next tourist fell from the cliff, hopefully executing a Reverse 2 1/2 Somersaults in the Pike Position, Jack decided that he would use the occasion to clean up the Yellow.

Thud.

A brilliant yellow light shone like a beacon that no one wanted to see.

"What the f—," said a local.

The local crushed his can of High Power in his fist. He threw the can into the small stream that flowed away from the waterfall and into the Meandering River, which spun like a corkscrew in a polluted bottle all the way down to hell.

Jack's ruse had not worked. Locals were immune to the tourists that fell like water from the cliff. Tourists falling from the cliff were like waking up each day and not wanting to go back to work. The dream of another cold can of High Power faded into reality and became a real can of High Power right there on the breakfast table.

Jack should have known better.

"Call the Rangers!" said the local. "It's that asshole from the nuthouse! Flashing his yellow dick!"

The ghost of Sid began to growl and bark, but no one could hear him, let alone see him.

Tourists who had not yet climbed the sandstone steps to the edge of the cliff jumped from the shallow pool. Parents yanked their children from the water. The water had become radioactive like the sun.

Jack ran.

His feet dug into the spent cigarette butts and the cool sand on the floor of the cave.

The calluses of his feet waved goodbye.

Thud.

Another tourist fell from the cliff above Tourist Falls and landed like a cosmic body crashing into the earth. Jack stumbled over the irregular ground. Impact craters from past tourist-falling events impeded Jack's escape like an extinction record laid bare. Jack cut down into the creek and splashed through the shallow water like an alligator racing through time.

Locals set down their cans of beer and tried to call the Rangers, but there was no cell phone coverage at Tourist Falls. Jack reached his bicycle. He pedaled away on the rain-muddled path, and through the leaves, and over the hills, and back toward the hungry mouths of the Locavores.

"What happened?" asked the Revolutionary, back at the cave.

Out of breath and without most of his clothes or his bicycle, Jack said, "I popped a tire on the way back."

He grabbed his t-shirt from the grocery store raid and put it on. The Revolutionary handed him a pair of slacks.

"Where the hell did you get these?"

Jack wrapped his bed sheet around his shoulders and brewed a cup of tea. Then, he told the story of his bath.

He ended with, "so, I just left the bike in the woods. I felt bad about it, but it wasn't much use to me anymore."

"Aw," said Hippie Girl.

"You'll find another one," said the Revolutionary. "I've seen plenty of them around."

"Think the Rangers will be after us?" said Jack.

The Locavores looked at one another.

The dream of free local chickens for everyone evaporated in the Revolutionary's mind.

"O," said the Deep Breathers, "shit."

The Wood Fairies got all up in Jack's face and began hurling their typical vitriol at him.

"Do you know what will happen if those Rangers screw an un-punctured lid on our moonshine jar?" screamed the Wood Fairies. "No more fucking tea!"

Jack shuddered in the face of that void and from the cold all around him.

"Be vigilant," said the Revolutionary.

Milk Tick suckled at Hippie Girl's breast.

"Good idea," said Jack.

"All for a bath," said Hippie Girl. "Far out."

Hippie Girl lit up a spliff. She had already harvested her fall crop of weed.

The Silent Ethiopian remained silent.

The Locavores went to bed without their supper.

Jack had not gathered any acorns.

The next morning, the Rangers' phones began to ring like gunshots on opening day.

"Do you know what might happen?" said the Saber Rattler, on the phone with Ranger Four.

"Yeah, we do," said Ranger Four.

"Tourism will decline! Economic disaster! Tales of Yellow Woe!"

"Ten-Four," said Ranger Four.

"Well, then, do something!" said the Saber Rattler, who was very good at shaking things up.

"We will," said the Ranger.

"Maybe this guy could come over for a game of Risk sometime," said Ranger Two, who was listening in.

"Start asking around if anyone has anything on their trail cameras that might be helpful," said the Saber Rattler. "And check with those chicken farmers. The ones that lost a bunch of chickens."

The Saber Rattler whispered bold, loud words of Armageddon and fear and hung up the phone.

"I'll call the Law," said Ranger Four. "See if they've heard anything."

"Nah, let's give it a few more days," said Ranger Two. "I've got some ponds to think about stocking next spring. Not to mention deer season and Risk on Thursday."

"Ponds to stock and poachers to rock."

"Plus, I gotta dig those holes."

"Wednesday?"

"Yeah. Wanna help?"

"Damn, I hope I get Australia."

Ranger Four dialed the number of a chicken farmer who had called in after hours about damage to his old championship Demolition Derby station wagon.

"South America for me," said Ranger Two. "All the way."

TRAIL CAMERA

At the police station in town, a Lawman had just begun interrogating the bass player for the rocknrollers when another call came in about a broken-down truck full of holes.

"Okay, give me the lowdown," the Lawman was saying, when the phone rang.

The image of an arrow protruding from the metal chassis of an old car fluttered like PTSD before the Lawman's eyes.

"Sons of bitches," said the Lawman. "Call in some Rangers."

On the other side of the county, Jack and the Revolutionary reigned in their imaginary horses. A late-model Lincoln Continental sat beside a perforated old stop sign at a long-abandoned intersection. A skeleton was slumped over the steering wheel inside the car, still waiting on traffic.

"WHOOP!" said the Pits.

What little air remained in the tire of the Lincoln exploded back into the atmosphere.

The Revolutionary nocked an arrow.

Wide-sweeping social change would have to wait.

At the Ranger's district headquarters, Ranger Four and Ranger Two were in the middle of a game of pin the tail on the coyote when the phone interrupted their fun.

"We need some help with these 'Locavores,'" said a Lawman. "First, it was the commotion in the grocery store, and now they're shooting up all the dead cars in the county."

"Ten-Four," said Ranger Four.

"We've had about all we can take," said the Lawman.

"Okay," said the Ranger.

"The Saber Rattler's getting mad," said the Lawman.

"Shit," said Ranger Four. "He called here just the other day."

"If I have to hear him whisper any more words of fear and Armageddon," said the Lawman, "I'm gonna start getting flashbacks."

The Lawman's thoughts spun backward anyway. Games of Risk, freewheeling drifters, rocknrollers, and the pack of dogs that he had slaughtered outside the Walls of Knowledge Library wound tightly to the reel of his brain. Then came his memories of war. The Lawmen didn't push play.

"Maybe we should dig a hole for him sometime," said Ranger Two, who was always listening in.

"I'm not fooling," said the Lawman. "You know they're out there in a cave somewhere. Isn't that a job for you Rangers?"

"Yeah, we'll find them. I called a few chicken farmers, but haven't come up with much on their location yet."

"It's that yellow-dick guy. From the nuthouse."

"Yeah, we know," said Ranger Four. "Fucking weirdo. We already put that guy away once. His goddamn dog about took off one of my hands."

"Jesus," said the Lawman. "I heard about that. And now there's talk of a gay gun."

"Gay gun?"

"Yeah," said the Lawman.

"What."

"In."

"The."

"Hell."

The Ranger said each word one at a time.

"We're meeting up with some locals at the Diner tomorrow morning," said the Lawman. "Said one of their trail cameras caught some hippie chick the other day staring into it for an hour giving it the peace sign. Might have some intel from some kids we just brought in as well. Why don't you fellas join us?"

"Ten-Four," said Ranger Four. "We'll have some guys there."

"And don't talk to the Saber Rattler," said the Lawman.

"We'll fill him in later."

"With dirt," said Ranger Two, under his breath.

"Copy that," said Ranger Four.

Ranger Four hung up the phone and picked up a pin.

"Whose turn is it?"

THE TEN CENT DINER

The next morning, Ranger Two and Ranger Six sat at a small table drinking weak black coffee, waiting for the Law. The Rangers wore muddy boots and green forest ranger outfits. Smokey the Bear wasn't with them, but he was in spirit. Smoking in public restaurants had been banned by the state for several years, and everyone at the Ten Cent Diner was still pissed about the legislation.

The bells attached to the front door of the diner ding-a-linged.

A pair of locals walked in.

The locals sat down on the worn black-cushioned chairs at the Rangers' table. They hooked their thumbs into their Carhartt jackets and scowled.

"Want some coffee?" asked the waitress.

"Nah," said the locals.

The locals smelled like Saturday night. They pulled out

some Snus and pushed it into their lips.

"We'll take a couple cups though."

The lazy waitress walked away.

"Now, about these 'Locavores' out in the woods," said a local, who had shit to do.

The Rangers' cold eyes narrowed into focus. They slurped their weak coffee. They wished that they carried guns.

"They best leave well enough alone," said the other local. Childhood memories of bedtime cut through the beer-brain fog in his mind. "All that carrying on out there. They don't want to be waking up no real Locavore. Some of them mines might of come unplugged by now."

"What with all the fracking."

"I've heard some of these stories," said Ranger Six, who was originally from Somewhere Else. "Some sort of mine monster? Jesus. This isn't bedtime. We've got bigger problems."

Ranger Two squirmed in his seat and took a drink of coffee.

The locals eyed each other.

"Gun season is coming up, as you fellas know," said Ranger Two, "and the Saber Rattler thinks these Locavores are gonna affect Tourism."

The lazy waitress shuffled over and set down the empty coffee cups.

"Goddamn fracking's gonna take care of that," she said. "I'll be back in a few hours if you all need a refill."

The lazy waitress walked back to the kitchen. She exited the diner through a door into an alley and chain-smoked cigarettes beside a bucket tagged:

Ranger Six sighed.

"Law says you fellas got a trail camera with some hippie chick on it," said Ranger Six.

The locals spit in their empty cups.

"Sure do. Had her breast hanging out with a kid nursing on it. Giving peace signs to the camera."

"She best not be scaring off those ten-pointers," said the other local.

"That's what I'm saying," said Ranger Two.

"Mr. Boyd, raises chickens down the way from my place," said the first local, "said he had a bearded guy on one of his cameras a while back. Had a bird dog with him. Marching around all weird."

The bells tinkled on the door of the Ten Cent Diner and the Sheriff and the Law walked in.

"Boys. I see you met the Rangers," said the Sheriff.

"Howdy," said the locals.

The Sheriff and the Lawmen pulled a table over and sat down.

"We busted some rocknrollers the other day for some future drugs," said a Lawman. "Trying to fly down Main

Street with their arms out. They had some interesting things to say about this hippie girl and that group she's with. Said they're living in some cave. Said they got their pot off this hippie girl."

"They won't last the winter in a cave," said the trail-camera local. He spit in his cup.

"They won't last the goddamn fall if I can help it," said the Sheriff. "Where the hell is that waitress?"

Out in Beetle Woods, the ground trembled, but it wasn't from fracking. Across the clearing, dozens of empty cans of Brush Lite rattled in the cold grass like aluminum maracas.

The front door of the diner chimed again.

"Nice bells," said a freewheeling drifter.

"Well, what do we have here?" said the Sheriff.

The planning stages for ridding the county of the Locavores turned as cold as the coffee in the Rangers' cups.

"Pull up a chair, son," said Ranger Two.

The freewheeling drifter was surprised that the Law was so friendly in this town.

"Yeah, thanks, that sounds great," said the freewheeling drifter. "I'm not leaving town for a few days."

"Ho, ho, yeah," said Ranger Two.

"Oh, we always have a great time," said a Lawman.

"Those Locavores can wait," said the Sheriff. "Ain't nobody driving those goddamn broken-down cars anyway."

"The Saber Rattler is gonna be pissed," said Ranger Six.

"That guy can shake his goddamn sword somewhere

else for a while," said the Sheriff. "Ain't nothing like a good game of Risk."

"Fucking 'Loca-bores' more like it," said a Lawman.

"Have you guys seen the waitress?" said the drifter.

The locals spit in their cups.

"But some of them cars is still good for the Derby," said the ten-point local.

The Demolition Derby was the highlight of his year.

"Shit," said the Sheriff, "You might be able to get one even cheaper then."

The Lawmen laughed.

"That's true," said the local.

"Slap on some Bondo and you're good to go," said the Sheriff.

The locals looked at each other again.

"I think we're done here," said the ten-pointer.

His cup was full.

The locals had better shit to do than worry about a bunch of freaks out in the woods or a fucking game of Risk.

They had beer to drink.

"Don't forget," said Ranger Two, to the freewheeling drifter, "Thursday night."

USHANKA

Once the cold air of late autumn hit the cave and didn't leave, the Revolutionary called another meeting to order.

"It's fucking cold," said the Revolutionary.

"No shit!" yelled the Wood Fairies, who could no longer collect their dew.

The Revolutionary pulled an ushanka hat from his cargo pocket and put it on.

"You fucking said it, Tommy!" said Tommy.

Frost plumed from the Deep Breathers' mouths like an alien volcano.

"From now on, we will abandon our righteous, but apparently pointless crusade against the broken-down cars of the county," said the Revolutionary. "And we will take up arms again against the deer, for we are hungry and in need of provision."

"Amen," said Megan.

"Totally," said Hippie Girl.

"It's about fucking time!" said the Wood Fairies.

"Besides, we are almost out of ammunition," said the Revolutionary. "We need food."

"We still have the tortilla chips," said Jack.

But no one answered. Hundreds of plastic bags of burnt tortilla chips lay stacked in the back of the cave like plastic bags full of burnt tortilla chips that no one wanted to eat.

Jack and the Revolutionary readied their gear for the hunt.

Jack sorted through the winter clothes that he and the Silent Ethiopian had stolen from the drop box in front of the thrift store in town.

The Silent Ethiopian warmed his hands over the smoldering fire of the mogogo.

"I bet the Silent Ethiopian is an amazing stalker," said Jack.

The Revolutionary pulled on the earflaps of his new hat.

"In the morning," said the Revolutionary, "we ride."

WALLACE STEVENS

The trees were cold. The few dead leaves that remained on the branches rattled like crisp mahogany gloves. This sound was remarkably loud in the crepuscular morning when nothing else yet moved but Jack. The sky hung heavy with the low clouds that had brought the powdery snow the night before. The clouds, like everything else, waited for the sun to warm them, so that they could begin to think about moving off again. Then dawn broke, and the steel sky streaked pink. A few small birds flitted in the skeletal brush. Squirrels itched the bark of large trees. Each sound moved freely through the sixteen-degree air.

Jack shivered. He had stopped on the edge of a field, unable to move farther without giving away his presence. The cold air shook him deep to the core, yet the movement was barely perceptible—a conservation of energy and heat.

The ghost of Sid sprung from nowhere and ran through

the field.

"Goddammit, Sid," said Jack. "Again?"

The ghost of Sid had never once spooked a deer. Jack couldn't figure it out, but it almost seemed as if the dog were not actually there.

Jack held the Pits across his body in the crook of his arm. His fingers pushed deep into the pockets of his coat, like coal miners within the earth.

"Wallace Stevens," said Jack.

The ghost of Sid bounded happily through the lightening air, no colder than any man.

WOODEN PEW

The doe stood fifty yards away chewing grass in the field. Sunlight had just begun to crest the ridge to the east. The Revolutionary had stalked the deer in the predawn morning for over an hour. In the darkness, there had been only the faint sounds of the deer—slow movements—grass torn from the earth—uncertainty. Then, with the light, gray masses taking form. The cold penetrated everything. Frost glittered across every blade of grass in the field, each ice crystal reflecting light like a mirror ball. The Revolutionary stumped forward on his knees. The ground reminded him of his childhood, kneeling on a wooden pew at Mass. The pew burned as if it were nailed to his knees. The doe chewed slowly. She watched, and she listened, and she stamped her foot when she sensed the presence of Man. Her children grew skittish at the stamping and hopped a barbed-wire fence into the woods. The Revolutionary waited. His nocked arrow lay in position across the riser of his bow—his fingers too cold to move. The wind began to stir with the warming of the earth, and Jack was too far off to help. The Revolutionary knew that he would never be able close the distance in the open field for a shot at the doe. With a snort, the doe spooked and jumped the fence after her progeny. Moving off quickly, the deer headed down into the still dark of the woods, like billy goats across a troll bridge to safety. Their shadow forms chewed on the last tender tips of greenbrier shoots and pulled what few leaves remained on the low branches. In the field above, the Revolutionary reconciled hope for change. The last of his cedar-shafted arrows gained moisture, and with it front-of-center balance, but none of that mattered now. The Revolutionary stood up. The stalk was over. Every fiber of muscle in his body relaxed against the cold and the single-minded focus of the hunt. He un-nocked his arrow from the bowstring and replaced it on his quiver. The day was lost.

DEAD ORANGE CREEK

Hippie Girl and Milk Tick looked at the orange water of the creek. The creek was dead. The water flowing in the creek was orange: Dead Orange Creek. Hippie Girl and Milk Tick skipped rocks across the icy-film that covered most of the surface of the creek. Hippie Girl threw a skipper that skipped thirty-seven times, breaking the thin ice along its path, until the rock clicked into another pile of rocks in the creek bed. Milk Tick threw a skipper that sunk immediately into the creek. Milk Tick had no technique. Milk Tick's small wrists had not yet developed the appropriate coordination for skipping rocks, but it was still fun to try.

"Fft, fft, fft," skipped the rocks.

"Plop," said Milk Tick's rock, as it snuggled into the bed.

Hippie Girl aimed for an embankment. Roots hung

through the dirt undercut by the creek like icicles in the unwashed hair of a warrior. Turtles and crawdads would have lived in this embankment if anything lived in Dead Orange Creek, but nothing did. The water was too sulfurous from the acid mine run-off from the one hundred and eleven gob piles and forty-seven abandoned coal mines that ran the length of the creek. Eventually, Dead Orange Creek emptied its dead water into the Meandering River, which then carried that water far away into the Mississippi Delta and then down into hell.

"Fft," went the rock, into the water destined for hell.

The Devil drank sulfurous tea; the Devil drank Dead Orange Creek. The Devil waited in the Mississippi Delta of the Mind, and his fingernails were all the dead creeks of the world.

LOVE

The Revolutionary stood on an oak ridge, and he was alone, except the world all around him. He sang his fake-Indian totem song:

> *"I am a shark*
> *I will catch you*
> *I am a killer*
> *I will get you*
> *I am a shark*
> *I am a killer*
> *I will catch you*
> *I will get you.*
>
> *I am a shark*
> *I will catch you*
> *I am a killer*

Bram Riddlebarger

I will get you
I am a shark
I will catch you
I will get you
I will eat you."

The Revolutionary repeated this mantra over and over. The words swept through the steep, short valley. Every deer within one hundred yards ran away. Wild turkeys played their own game, and Man was only sometimes in it. The squirrels hit pause.

Merle Haggard did, too.

The Revolutionary felt serious.

It was a strange perspective that overcame him in moments of natural wonder—the splendor of joy.

O, Hippie Girl.

They were not made to last.

The dream was almost over.

MOUND

Jack and the Revolutionary sat on a mound. The mound was out in the woods, and not terribly large, and small trees grew out of the mound like hairs. The mound was an earthworks left over from a Native American culture that no one could remember.

"Deep within this mound," said the Revolutionary, "are the bones of our forefathers."

Jack looked at the Revolutionary.

"I thought you were from Iowa."

"Never mind," said the Revolutionary. "What we seek is a return to the pagan—to the hills—to a life without cars."

The Revolutionary fiddled with the chert-tipped arrow that rested on the shelf of his bow.

"Maybe we shouldn't sit here," said Jack.

"Don't ever tell," said the Revolutionary.

"Yeah, those college kids would probably come out and

dig this shit up," said Jack.

"No," said the Revolutionary.

"What?" said Jack.

"Don't tell that I'm from Iowa," said the Revolutionary.

"Oh," said Jack.

"I don't think I have much weight left to lose."

"At least there's still tea," said Jack.

Sid ran up to the Revolutionary and nuzzled his hand. Sid had been chasing chipmunks, which darted like arrows not equipped with Judo points into the leaves and hollows of old logs. Sid licked the Revolutionary's outstretched hand and looked deep within the Revolutionary to where Sid believed the connection would be made that had no voice but which required his master to pet his belly.

The dead leaves fell from the deep autumn trees.

"You ever been to Serpent Mound?" asked the Revolutionary.

"No, but I've heard of it."

"It's a mound in the shape of a serpent," said the Revolutionary. "It must be several hundred yards long."

"Maybe the same people that built this mound."

"No one knows who built it," said the Revolutionary. "Or how. Or even why."

"Weird," said Jack.

"The snake is eating an egg," said the Revolutionary. "A dirt egg. Or maybe it's meant to be the world."

"I could probably eat a dirt egg right now," said Jack.

"Eating the world," said the Revolutionary. He picked up a twig and broke it into small pieces.

"It seems like a lot of work," said Jack. "Wooden shovels

and shit. Think how long it would take just to make this one we're sitting on. There isn't even much topsoil here anyway. Why cooperate?"

"Hippie Girl thinks it's some zodiac shit," said the Revolutionary. He pulled on his beard.

"Maybe it's the sign of a monster," said Jack. "Like some horror movie omen."

"Probably just some rich asshole chieftain that wanted to leave his mark," said the Revolutionary. "Like a fucking skyscraper."

"A dirtscraper," said Jack.

The autumn air blew. The Revolutionary tossed the small broken pieces of the twig, like bones, onto the mound.

"I'm cold," said Jack. "The Pits is, too."

"Let's go shoot some cars," said the Revolutionary. "One last time."

"I've only got a few rounds left," said Jack.

"And then we'll get some tea," said the Revolutionary.

Jack and the Revolutionary stood up and walked away from the mound in the woods that contained the stratified remains of a culture that no one would ever remember.

INDIAN SUMMER

Hippie Girl needed a bath. Not a soap-and-bubbles-in-an-enameled-tub-for-long-steamy-hours-with-many-candles-bath, but something close to it: rubbing down in a waterfall. Jack's foray to Tourist Falls had planted the mental seed in her mind, and that seed had sprouted into need.

Rangers be damned.

The cold weather broke around a full moon. A few days of Indian summer were common during the winter months in the foothills of Appalachia. Hippie Girl snuck out of the cave and away from Milk Tick's eternal lock on her nipple. Milk Tick was full. She would be safe, nuzzled up against Sid and the Revolutionary. Hippie Girl made her way through the shadows in the light of the moon. She toked her magic as she walked. The cold had returned during the night, but the break in the season was not yet gone. The water would still be like ice on her skin.

Hippie Girl arrived at Tourist Falls in the small hours of the morning. The rate of tourists falling from the cliff had dropped significantly from the tourist bustling afternoons and weekends of the summer and autumn, but that rate picked up again when Hippie Girl took off her dress in the light of the moon.

Hippie Girl stepped into the shallow pool at the base of the waterfall. The bracing water cleansed her. Bodies and water fell. She thought of the cave and the Locavores and Milk Tick back against the Revolutionary's warm body. Milk Tick was probably ready for milk, but then it was just the falling water on her skin.

An aging male tourist cannonballed off the cliff and into the pool ninety feet below, crushing his legs up into his skull.

This was as clean as the water would be.

Hippie Girl sighed, and the water fell over her sore nipples like lanolin in the light of the full moon. Her breasts were swollen—full of milk for Milk Tick, the miracle. She stood in the pool at the base of the waterfall and looked up at the falling water. The water fell like LSD, sharp as it hit her skin. The water coursed down through her curly-blonde hair and then down over her breasts and then ran cold through her pubic hair and down to her toes in the pool of the waterfall. Hippie Girl relaxed. The cold of the water in the dark morning hardened her sore nipples. She reached down and between her legs and up and down and slowly up and down, and she felt at home in the falling water of the world and the pleasure and the release from the cave, as the bodies crashed to the earth in the sandstone sand of

Tourist Falls.

She shuddered violently in the shallow pool. She squatted down and rinsed herself and stepped from the water. The exploded body of a tourist lay atop the hem of her dress. She pulled it from the mess and ran, frigid now in the air, back to the cave and to Milk Tick, and to the Locavores uncertain future.

TORTILLA CHIPS

The squirrels and worms and deer and other creatures of the forest had finished off most of the acorns. All that remained for food in the cave were the bags and plastic bags full of tortilla chips.

The tortilla chips were made by a local company and sold in stores around the town. The tortilla chip company obtained their corn from the fields of small-time farmers in the county who were not occupied with the production of chickens. After the harvest, the company sent the corn to another company far upstate in order for that company to convert the corn into crunchy tortilla chips. The chip-making company promptly converted the corn that was sent to them into nixtamal, and then into masa, and then into burnt tortilla chips. The chip-making company had all the necessary equipment to make burnt tortilla chips. They packaged the tortilla chips in clear plastic bags. Delivery trucks hauled them back to the town. There, the bags were placed on shelves and racks to sell to fools that bought burnt local tortilla chips that were processed Somewhere Else.

The manager of the grocery store wasn't impressed. He had given local a try, but shelf space was money.

Under the Revolutionary's direction, the Locavores had collected hundreds of bags of the tortilla chips from the grocery store dumpster the night after their invasion into the produce section, but no one would eat them. The plastic bags sat against a wall in the back of the cave like nuts that couldn't be cracked.

Unable to find enough food around them, the Locavores began to starve.

SQUIRRELS

"Why don't we get some squirrels?"

"You ever tried to hit a squirrel with an arrow?"

"No."

"Well, I have. Fuckers are fast. Plus, I lost a bunch of arrows."

"I could try with the Pits."

"Fifty-caliber on a squirrel?"

"Well, I could try."

"You wouldn't find it if you hit it."

SCORCHED EARTH

"I've heard there's some sort of tree around here that we could eat the pods off of," said Hippie Girl, once the Locavores could only sit around the cave and dream of food.

"Yeah? Dogwood?" Jack guessed.

Sid perked up his ears.

"Redbud," said the Revolutionary. "It's redbud."

The Revolutionary had a mind like a red trap.

"Righteous," said Hippie Girl. "Redbud. I could go for some of that right now." She took a toke of her tea. The sumac lemonade was long gone.

"I think we might have to wait till spring," said the Revolutionary.

The Locavores looked out of the cottonmouth of the cave. Tan seedpods dangled on the branches of the sycamore trees, like inedible Christmas ornaments hanging from a tree with no presents beneath it. The evening panorama had not changed for weeks.

The only thing red in the winter before them was the occasional flash of a woodpecker.

"Well, I'm hungry," said Hippie Girl. "Milk Tick is, too. Here, Milk Tick."

Milk Tick latched on.

"Tk, tk, tk, tk, tk," said Milk Tick.

The rest of the Locavores drank their teas and considered finally eating the burnt tortilla chips.

"Those tortillas chips are like the scorched-earth policy of hunger," said the Revolutionary.

The Locavores went to bed, and their bellies rumbled, like tanks over the hard, cold ground of winter.

SATAN IS REAL

"You must cook a sauce long and slow," said the Revolutionary.

"I've heard that," said Jack.

He and the Revolutionary had risen early and gone out looking for something to forage. They had not found any food.

They were back at the small mound.

They sat and watched the dead leaves blow in the beech trees. The leaves were brown and withered. The moment was almost up.

"There's nothing worse than weak sauce," said the Revolutionary.

"Well, there are those tortilla chips," said Jack.

"At least they aren't yellow."

Snow began to fall, pushed sideways by the wind.

"You know, there was a time when I ate beans at every

meal," said the Revolutionary.

They were so hungry that the idea of beans didn't constrict their stomachs, so much as it implied a great cataclysm of social revolution.

"We tried," said the Revolutionary.

"I could use some tea," said Jack.

"It's hard out here when you are still on the frontier," said the Revolutionary.

"Fuck," said Jack.

A few dead leaves fell and spun pirouettes to the earth with the snow.

The Revolutionary thought of Hippie Girl when she was still happy and full of energy.

"There is only one direction," said the Revolutionary. "Forward."

The men sat and thought of the things that men think about when they are hungry and cold and the future is before them.

The cold wind blew.

They were at peace in a troubling world.

"Where do we go from here?" asked Jack.

The Revolutionary was silent.

His treatise had an end.

"I see now that Satan is real," said Jack.

Merle Haggard switched to a cover of the Louvin Brothers.

"Why is that?" said the Revolutionary, after a time.

"Because it is everything that condemns us to further solitude," said Jack.

The leaves settled down into grave blankets covered in

snow.

The mound below them did not respond.

SMARTPHONE JESUS

Things got weird in the cave when the Revolutionary pulled out his smartphone. Then, everyone else did, too, except Jack. Jack didn't have a phone. If he had had a phone, he wouldn't have had anyone to call or to text anyway. But the other Locavores had acquired the phones, seemingly from nowhere, in an act that rivaled the Second Coming in reverse. Something was lost, and gained.

"You guys have phones?" said Jack.

The ghost of Sid hovered in the cave, and the air moved around. The air smelled like fungus. It was randy and alive.

Tip, tip, tip. Tap, tap, tap. Tip, tip, tip.

The cave transformed into a sonic finger dance of concentration.

The Silent Ethiopian tapped, too, but his phone was on mute.

Maybe I could get a phone in town and text myself, thought

Jack. *I could text myself and reply and generate an entire novel, like a psychological treatise on thought and stagnation.*

Radioactive electrical vibes ran through the Black Hand Sandstone of the cave, and through the dander and the dust. The mogogo went cold.

Resonance—deep into deep—world into world—cell into cell.

Tip, tip, tip. Tap, tap, tap. Tip, tip, tip.

You could not stop it, Russia.

The earth rumbled.

THE PLOT

"So, that's it then?" asked Hippie Girl, several days before the Revolutionary left the cave.

"I move to the land of cars," said the Revolutionary.

"They will shake your hands."

"They will lumber mechanically to the lake and drink."

"They will slide off roads and kiss trees."

"They will come and, coming, I will hear them come, and their weight will give them away."

THE END OF THE REVOLUTIONARY

The Revolutionary rolled from the floor of the cave, grabbed his hunting knife, and shaved off his beard. The hairs left his face like peasants pulled from their homes during a long war of snowy attrition.

"Borsht face!" screamed the Wood Fairies, when they saw the horror.

The Revolutionary had remembered that his name was Jeff.

He took off his clothes.

"Give me back the slacks," he said.

Jack and the Revolutionary traded pants.

Jeff quickly left the cave. He was going back to Iowa. He didn't walk or ride an imaginary horse to get there; he drove.

Jeff was ready to resume his high school teaching career.

The ghost of Sid popped out of existence, and Sid

regrouped to Jack's side. Hippie Girl smoked a doobie. She wondered how long she could keep hanging out in the cave with the remaining Locavores and the ghost of the Revolutionary.

"That fucking loser!" shrieked the Wood Fairies, when it was obvious that Jeff was not coming back.

Hippie Girl's patterned dress ruffled in the draft that blew in from the cold mouth of the sandstone outcropping that the Locavores had been calling a cave all this time.

This dress could use a washboard, thought Hippie Girl, as she held Milk Tick close.

The rekindled mogogo lent a terrible smell to the cave.

"Poor Milk Tick," said Hippie Girl.

EXODUS

"We're leaving," said Hippie Girl.

"About time!" said the Wood Fairies.

"I'm going back to work," said Megan.

"Milk Tick is full," said Hippie Girl.

"Bloated," said the Wood Fairies.

"Teething is painful," said the dental hygienist.

"O," said the Deep Breathers.

Silence from the Silent Ethiopian.

"We're tired of living in this cave," said Career Woman.

"We're growing up," said Milk Kid.

"She'll need to begin to floss soon," said the hygienist.

"Take a deep breath," said the twins.

"Goodbye," said the Ethiopian.

"Write sometime. We'll be in Portland," said Kathy.

"Lol," said Fiona.

"I need a High Power," said Megan.

"We can breathe again," said Eric and Tim.

"Later," said Addisu.

The Wood Fairies were not even real.

This was the end of the Old Way.

This was the end of the Locavores.

Only the legend of the Locavore remained, like Mothman on the Silver Bridge of the town's collective mind.

Everyone left the cave, except Jack and Sid.

No one waved.

"Goodbye," said Jack.

Sid wanted to go along.

The thought of canned dog food for his worn teeth made his tail wag. No more leaves for a bed. No more dirty paws from digging a hole for rest. Less fear. The tranquility of endless days within a house, as the birds twilled through clear panes of glass fit snugly into their frames. The rigidity of a schedule.

But no one wanted a new, old dog.

"Just you and me again, buddy," said Jack.

Dust motes floated around him.

"And the Yellow."

Jack poured himself a cup of tea.

ASCENSION

She rose up like the Virgin Mary carved from watermelon light.

"Whoa."

Kathy ascended into heaven. She never made it to Portland. It was the heaven of Everything.

"It's the future," said Kathy.

She had finally taken the future drugs.

"Whoa," said Kathy, again.

Her Birkenstocked feet would not be back on the ground.

Fiona stayed behind.

Fiona's place was on the earth.

WINTER

"I'm living off the fat of the land, man," said Jack.

Sid stood in the middle of their couch with a baleful look, as if deep in his dog eyes another man sat before him.

Their couch was a large pile of dead leaves piled close to the mogogo.

For Sid, the absence of the Revolutionary felt like the loss of chicken.

Jack nestled down into the leaves with his bed sheet and ate a boiled acorn.

The deep winter had come.

It was too cold to hunt.

Jack had found a few acorns that the squirrels had missed.

He stood up and warmed his cup of tea over the nearly imperceptible glow emanating from the coals under the mogogo. He had burned through his wood supply. Any deadfall that he collected now was ripped from the frozen ground and wet. Jack sat back down on his leaf couch. He held his last boiled acorn like the final sheet on a roll of toilet paper. He had to make this one count.

"Fucking acorns," said Jack.

DANDRUFF

Snow dusted the road like dandruff on the shoulder of an old man's coat.

"I'm sick of winter," said Jack.

He held the Revolutionary's recurve bow in his cold hand. He had used up the last of the muzzleloader's sabot rounds blasting a broken-down pickup truck's windows to smithereens. Some habits, unlike windows, were hard to break.

The Pits was back in the recess of the cave.

Jeff had left the bow behind when he returned to his academic duties and to life without a cave.

Jack fiddled with one of the reed-shafted arrows. He could barely draw the bow, let alone shoot it.

A deep chill had set in his bones.

The mystique of the Revolutionary's war against the automobiles had faded. Jack was starving and cold. He placed the arrow on the riser. The end of the bison-cars was really just the end of his ammunition.

The sun shot golden rays of radiation into space, like a night without sleep.

Sid sniffed at a half-crushed can of Brush Lite beside the road.

"Sid, move," said Jack.

Jack nocked the arrow. The Revolutionary had fitted this arrow with the last of his Judo points. Judo points were good for practice shooting, because the small metal arms on the point prevented the shaft from burying the arrow too deeply when the point struck the ground.

Jack drew the bow and loosed the arrow well below the draw weight of the bow.

"Thwack!" said the arrow.

Ice crystals shattered on the ground like a cosmos too far off to see.

Jack missed the can by three feet.

"Wallace Stevens," said Jack.

The snow dusted the road.

Spring was far away.

BONES IN THE EARTH

Sid stood on the dead leaves of the couch and drooled. The tumor on his belly waited with pursed lips to kiss the sand and the dander on the floor of the cave.

"She was homely, but welcoming," said Jack.

Jack missed the Locavores, especially Hippie Girl.

After they left, Jack had taken the Wood Fairies' moonshine jar from the cave and thrown it as far as he could into the woods. It landed with an unbroken thud and bounced once.

"Goddammit," said Jack. "This goddamn Yellow."

TUMOR

The tumor on Sid's belly had begun as a small lump. Then the lump became a big lump, and then a giant lump, and then a lump that made no one want to pet the dog. After that, it became a belly-hanging pouch of certain death. Sid would totter from one place to the next—the cold air of the cave, the knee-deep snow, the dead leaves of the world. Jack wrapped his bed sheet around him.

And before long, there was just the ghost of Sid again, but this ghost was just a memory.

And Jack was alone.

INTERLUDE: THE
LONESOME FUGITIVE

Merle Haggard's "Sing A Sad Song" takes us home.

DAFFODILS

The purple of the iris still hid belowground. The daffodils had come up early, as usual, prematurely announcing glad yellow tidings, but they would hang their yellow heads for a few weeks more, swaying in the cold t-shirt wind under the low clouds, like Jesus' head hanging on the cross.

"I hate daffodils," said Jack. "Goddamn yellow."

Jack trudged back to the cave from his foraging expedition. He couldn't believe that he had made it through the winter. His supply of spicebush for his herbal tea was nearly gone, but he had added some early-sprouting ramps, chickweed, and non-flowering trout lily to his diet.

Jack had stolen a book on edible plants from the Walls of Knowledge Library.

Why didn't I think of this sooner, he thought, as he snuck past a high-school volunteer librarian, who was dusting an empty shelf.

Back in the cave, Jack sat on the leaf-couch and thumbed through the book. He sipped his tea. In the back of his throat, the taste of a winter's worth of burnt tortilla chips involuntarily made him wretch.

"Should be a lot better soon," said Jack.

But the Locavore had awoken.

AWAKENING

The Locavore pushed the blue, arrow-studded VW Beetle from the ground, like a cork leaving a bottle, and crawled to the surface. Ancient mine timbers and trolley cars full of coal slag erupted from the ground behind the Beetle like the detonated nest of a carnivorous bird. Beer cans were flattened. The Locavore was immense. The Beetle pinwheeled across the dead grass of the field and landed with its tires spinning in the air. Arrow shafts snapped, and the silver VW hubcaps rolled away like quarters across a table.

The Locavore knew what it had to do.

Its time had come.

CROCUS

"I'm trying to remember why the fuck I'm here."

Jack stood just below an oak ridgeline with the Revolutionary's bow crooked in his arm. He was leaning against a butternut tree that he had mistaken for an oak.

Below Jack's vision, nothing moved. He waited for something to appear, but nothing did.

Occasionally, a squirrel would bitch about Jack being there or a chipmunk would scamper from the leaves and then dart back into a log. A few woodpeckers lived their graceful, stuttering lives, beautiful flashes of red in the still gray of the woods. Life was peaceful, and nothing moved.

Spring had come.

Something stirred.

It was not a crocus.

ATTAINMENT

The monster strode through the woods, crippling small trees and pissing off squirrels, on a virtual beeline toward the power that it could now fully feel. The earth did not quite shake as its hideous feet struck the ground, but tremors of girth radiated from the shock. There was no thought in the monster's brain, only instinct and will.

The Locavore found Jack alone and freezing inside the cave. No steam arose from the cup of herbal tea that sat beside him. The spring evening had turned cold and frozen again. The Locavore entered the cave and smashed the mogogo back into clay. Jack saw the monster, but he could not move. The Locavore picked Jack up from his couch of powdered leaves and carried him out of the cave and into the open air. On the horizon, the yellow sun set without a trace of heat. The Locavore stripped the filthy clothes off Jack and ripped the golden rod from his body.

Bram Riddlebarger

And with it, the monster tore the face from the earth.